Olympic Vista Chronicles

Songs from the Wood

Book Two

Kelly Pawlik

Acknowledgements

Many thanks to: Emily, Bonnie, Darren, Mike, Tina, Maggie, Ken, and Darcy.

For permission, please email
olympicvistapublishing@gmail.com
Website: olympicvistapublishing.com

Bookstores and wholesale orders can be placed through
olympicvistapublishing@gmail.com

Cover art design: Greta Paliulyte

Sequel to: *Yesterday's Gone* (Olympic Vista Chronicles Book One)

Pawlik, Kelly, author
Issued in print and electronic formats
ISBN 978-1-7777181-3-8 (paperback)
ISBN 978-1-7777181-4-5 (epub)

DISCLAIMER
This is a work of fiction. Any names and characters are used fictitiously or are the product of the author's imagination. Any resemblance to actual persons, living or dead, is entirely coincidental.

OLYMPIC VISTA
PUBLISHING

This book is dedicated
to Adelaide and Darius.
You may not be flesh and bone,
but my adventures with you are real.

One

Amidst the cacophony of jeers, laughter and friendly banter, the silence in the front most bench of the school bus was deafening. It was early morning and the front lawns and gardens sparkled with morning dew. The school year had only recently begun and most of the students were still excited for the potential the next ten months held. The pleasant-faced driver pulled the yellow school bus onto the side of the road and opened the door to let the final batch of students climb aboard.

Adelaide tucked her long brown hair behind her ear as she stared out the window. Her black leather wrist cuff, studded with black and white squares, peeked out from the sleeve of her denim jacket. She wore her usual solemn expression as she admired a garden alive with echinacea. Adelaide had no idea what the pink flower was called, but she wondered how it would look in her own yard. Once the new arrivals were safely seated, the bus continued its trek down the streets of Olympic Vista toward James Morrison Elementary School.

"Won't you talk to me? Normally?" Tetsu begged. He sat slumped in the seat beside Adelaide. Behind him, their friend Kurt shook his head, amused.

"Isn't this *normal?*" Adelaide asked with a strange cadence to her voice. She plastered a fake smile across her face before she turned and looked at her best friend. A few days ago, Tetsu had suggested Adelaide's usual monotone voice made her sound like a robot. While she'd heard similar comments from people in the past, his words wounded her, and she wasn't ready to forgive him. "It is," —she paused for emphasis— "what *you* wanted. Isn't *it?*"

Tetsu slumped further into his seat. "It really isn't."

The clear sky had already started to cloud over as the bus pulled up to its usual spot outside the sprawling, one-storey, beige building. A large white sign with black letters spelled out James Morrison Elementary School. Students collected their bags and pushed their way to the exit as the bus doors opened. Adelaide, who preferred a seat at the front of the bus, was one of the first students off. She left without looking at Tetsu and made her way toward the covered area of the school grounds.

"Adelaide!" Julie called as she exited the bus a few people behind Adelaide. Like most of the girls in their grade, Julie wore vibrant skirts and matching tops. Today she was dressed in a neon pink skirt and sweatshirt.

Julie didn't live in Adelaide's neighbourhood and had boarded the bus several stops prior to Adelaide's stop. Sophie, who did live on the same street as Adelaide, usually sat with Julie on the bus. While Sophie often spent time with Adelaide, Tetsu, and Kurt outside of school, she had dedicated this year to being popular. Popularity did not follow Kurt or Tetsu around, but today it seemed to follow Adelaide.

Adelaide stopped and turned. Julie and Sophie approached her. The two girls walked in step with each other and Adelaide tried not to frown.

"I'm so excited about this weekend," Julie prattled. "I think your mom is just the best! Will that cool guy with the cowboy hat be there?"

"Waylon?" Adelaide's brow furrowed. "He's our roommate."

"It's so *cool* that you have roommates." Julie flicked her crimped brown hair over her shoulder.

"Okay," Adelaide said, confused. "When will he be where?"

Julie giggled in response.

Adelaide gritted her teeth at the noise. She turned and searched Sophie's face, but Sophie refused to meet her gaze. Tetsu and Kurt joined the trio of girls.

Julie turned as a shiny black Lincoln Town Car pulled into the parking lot. Everyone else's gaze followed. They watched as Davia Belcouer climbed out of the passenger's side. Her butter yellow blouse, which had lacy frills down the front, was tucked into her jeans. She wore shiny black shoes and a pair of socks that matched her top. Her long blond hair was coiffed like the models in the latest issue of *Teen Beat*. She slung a jean jacket over her shoulder and closed the car door.

While everyone else stared at Davia's exit from the car, Adelaide's gaze fell on Darius, who got out of the back seat. Davia and her slightly older twin brother had moved from Boston with their parents at the end of the summer. Both of them had faint Boston accents, but that seemed to be where their similarities ceased. Where Davia strived to be popular, Darius was more determined to have fun and explore the strangeness of Olympic Vista. A smile played at Adelaide's lips as she recalled sneaking out of her house to investigate a so-called haunted house at Darius' suggestion. The entire adventure had left the group with more questions than answers.

Darius' eyes were wide and hungry for excitement as he looked about the schoolyard. They made Adelaide yearn for something she couldn't quite describe. Her cheeks flushed and she looked down at the ground as he caught sight of her.

"I love her clothes," Julie murmured.

Sophie sighed and rolled her eyes.

Although Davia was new to the school this year, she had already proved herself to be one of the most popular girls at school, much to Sophie's dismay. Last night Adelaide, Kurt, and Tetsu had listened to Sophie lament about Davia in the Hideout, a room in the basement of Sophie's house.

Adelaide looked up as Darius made his way across the parking lot toward them. He gave her a big wave and an even bigger grin.

"She killed a person, you know," Tetsu said. His words interrupted everyone's thoughts.

"What?" Julie gasped as they all turned to look at him.

"Davia. She killed a person, but she's too young and rich to go to jail." He nodded knowingly.

"Yeah, that's true." Sophie followed Tetsu's lead.

"I have to warn people," Julie gulped. She turned and ran off to another group of students nearby.

"That was mean," Adelaide said in her usual tone.

Tetsu shrugged. The four of them watched as Davia approached Farrah Turner, last year's most popular female sixth grader. Farrah's blond hair had also been teased and sprayed to perfection. Today she wore her rhinestone jean jacket. If the most popular girl this year wasn't Davia, it would be Farrah.

***

Darius grinned at Adelaide as he joined the circle of friends in front of the school. Adelaide's lips curved slightly and offered a small smile back.

"What's going on guys?" Darius asked.

"Tetsu is up to no good," Adelaide said in her deadpan voice.

Darius frowned at Tetsu.

"Come on." Sophie tilted her head to the side with an imploring look at Adelaide. "That was funny."

"Only until it catches up with you both," Adelaide warned them. She turned to Darius. "Want to walk? You can come too, Kurt."

Kurt brushed his reddish-brown hair out his eyes and looked between Adelaide and Darius, Sophie and Tetsu. Darius smiled at him. Of all of Adelaide's friends,

Kurt was his favourite. He reminded Darius of Quinton, a boy from Wiltshire Preparatory Academy back in Boston. The two hadn't been friends exactly, but Darius had stepped in when classmates bullied him.

"See you guys," Kurt said to Sophie and Tetsu as he fell in step with Darius and Adelaide.

Darius hadn't been able to stop thinking about the house he, Adelaide, and the rest of the group had investigated last week. As far as they could tell, a mad scientist or two had attempted to make their own Frankenstein's monster in the basement of an otherwise deserted house. After Darius and his new friends drew attention to the building, the authorities had intervened.

Darius had kept an eye on the paper ever since, but there had been no mention of an arrest. The most he could find was one tiny article that mentioned the police had been called to an abandoned house in town. If the authorities covered up the dead bodies in basements, Darius reasoned there were even more mysteries to unravel in the small town.

"Maybe we should look into that bird man," Darius proposed. He was desperate to find something else to investigate. His breath hitched as he recalled how alive he'd felt when he explored the haunted house. Adelaide had seemed as invested as he was. And they'd held hands under the table in the kitchen. He wanted to spend more time with her.

"Grover Jergen?" Adelaide asked. "I don't even know where we'd start."

"We could check other newspapers for signs of aggressive birds outside of Olympic Vista. Maybe he's gone farther afield. Or we could try to track down his family," Darius suggested.

"Good ideas." Adelaide nodded. "But if those agents we saw at the house are on the lookout for him, we probably won't get to him before they do."

"I still can't believe you two broke into a government building and looked at secret documents." Kurt shook his head. "I'm afraid Adelaide is probably right, though. I suspect they have vaster resources than either of you."

Darius turned and smiled at Kurt. "You really do read a lot, don't you?"

Kurt's cheeks turned pink. "I guess so," he mumbled.

"Sorry, Kurt. I didn't mean to embarrass you. It's a good thing," Darius assured him. He thought about the envelope he and Adelaide had found inside the office building and about all the other information that must be stored inside those walls. He desperately wished he still had the key card he'd stolen from the agent's car, but he knew Adelaide had been right to make him leave it behind in the office building.

The school bell rang and they filed inside.

***

It was mid-morning and Adelaide's classmates fidgeted at their desks. Their teacher, Mr. McKenzie, had been reviewing the multiplication tables and very few students enjoyed it.

Adelaide's stomach rumbled. She hoped no one noticed. Her mother had forgotten to get groceries again and the brown banana and stale rice cake Adelaide scavenged for breakfast hadn't done much to fill her stomach.

"And just before recess, let's talk current events," Mr. McKenzie said to the class. "As you all know, I encourage you to read the newspaper. It's important to be aware of what's going on. Can anyone give me some examples of things going on right now?"

A girl named Heather put up her hand.

"Yes, Heather?" Mr. McKenzie asked.

Adelaide thought she detected a hint of surprise in his tone.

"Whitney Houston won at the MTV music awards," Heather offered.

"That is current events. Thank you, Heather. Anyone else?" Mr. McKenzie asked.

The room filled with silence.

"All right, well, for example, it looks like some local flocks of birds are becoming increasingly territorial. Do any of you recall when Pine Park closed late this summer for a short time?"

A few people put up their hands, Adelaide included. She sensed Darius, who was often attentive in class, sit up straighter.

"Very good! You followed the news." Mr. McKenzie smiled.

"No," Brody said. "My neighbour told me about it. A bird snatched a whole apple right out of her hand. She screamed really loud when it flapped in her face. Made me glad I stayed home and played video games all summer." Brody wore a grim smile.

"And thank you for that, Brody." Mr. McKenzie's mouth formed a tight smile as he nodded. "Fresh air is good for you, but I'm glad you weren't the victim of a fowl mugging at the park." Mr. McKenzie paused for dramatic effect. "Anyone? No?"

Adelaide chuckled quietly to herself. Mr. McKenzie winked at her.

"All right then." Mr. McKenzie opened his mouth to carry on when another student put his hand up. "Yes?" Mr. McKenzie nodded in the student's direction.

"That's not exactly current though, Mr. McKenzie," Reggie pointed out.

"Thank you, Reggie. I'm getting there. It seems there was another similar incident just outside Seattle."

The bell rang and students shoved their books into their desks.

"Take it how you will, students," Mr. McKenzie said. "I'm not sure if we should put out bird feeders to placate them or just be wary. Go! Enjoy your recess." He waved them to freedom.

"We could stay inside and play video games," Brody suggested. "That would be safer."

"Video games can't be the solution to everything, Brody." Mr. McKenzie chuckled. "Off you go!"

Adelaide felt bad for Brody. He was a bulky kid, the kind of boy who would either grow into his size or forever be called names by his peers. Brody had sausage fingers and chubby cheeks, and his short-cropped hair made his head look too big for his body. He smelled vaguely of meatloaf and body odour.

Brody didn't have a lot of friends, so last year Adelaide had taken care to be extra nice to him. She'd greeted him before school and said goodbye at the end of the day. She'd been rewarded with her initials next to his. According to several people who sat next to him, Brody doodled "AW + BT" all over his notebooks and surrounded them with a heart.

Adelaide hadn't said anything about it, but it made her uncomfortable and she hadn't been quite as friendly to him since.

Running shoes squeaked against the floor as the students migrated to the playground and field. There was the usual hum of conversation, but Adelaide's attention was on Darius. He walked alongside her and she caught a whiff of pine and sandalwood, which she'd come to associate with him.

Adelaide inhaled through her nose and savoured the smell.

"I bet it's Grover Jergen!" Darius exclaimed. "I didn't see the article because I only looked at the local paper." He grimaced. "I should have looked at other papers."

Adelaide nodded. She suspected Darius was correct, but she wasn't sure how they could go investigate in Seattle.

"Maybe Farrah will be at the party," Tetsu teased Kurt as they passed through the school doors and spilled out onto the school grounds. "You could kiss her." Tetsu puckered his lips.

"Shut up," Kurt mumbled. He looked down at the ground and kicked a rock.

"What's this party everyone is talking about?" Darius asked.

"Yes, what is this party?" Adelaide echoed. She had almost forgotten her conversation with Julie earlier.

"Sophie told everyone you're having one." Tetsu shrugged. "I figured you knew. Part of this new you you've got going on."

Adelaide's hands turned clammy. A shiver ran down her spine and her vision blurred.

She felt like the world was being pulled out from under her feet and there was nothing to grab onto.

Two

Darius stood with his new friends outside the main doors of the school. He was irritated that Tetsu stood with them, but he kept it to himself. Adelaide still seemed upset with her friend and Darius wanted to protect her.

Everyone had started to talk about the party. Darius was excited at the idea, especially if Adelaide was going to be there. Now she was the host. Darius watched the colour drain from Adelaide's face and he knew he had to do something.

"I can host it at my house," Darius offered. He put his hand on Adelaide's arm. "We've got a pool house we can use. People can bring their swimsuits. I can take care of all the refreshments." He squeezed Adelaide's arm gently and willed her to look at him. "You'll come, right?"

"Sure, yes." Adelaide took a breath and her gaze met his. Her eyebrows knit together and Darius wanted to reach over and smooth them out. "Yes, I can be there," she continued in short bursts. "I can help. We can co-host. At your house." There was an edge of panic to her usually flat voice.

"What?" Tetsu gaped.

"Great!" Darius grinned and ignored Tetsu. He wanted to ask Adelaide if she was okay, or to reach over and hold her hand. Instead, he let go of her arm and changed the subject. "So, the bird attack near Seattle must be connected to the one that happened here. Did you see the one here? What do you know about it?"

"Why don't you go talk to Grody Brody and find out for yourself?" Tetsu jeered. "He seems to know somethin' about it. Maybe you could play video games with him after."

Darius took a deep breath and forced himself not to ball up his fists. He really didn't know what Tetsu's problem with him was, but as far as Darius was concerned, Tetsu certainly didn't seem to know how to treat his friends. "Did you apologize to Adelaide for whatever you did the other day?" Darius wheeled on Tetsu.

"I—"

"Then maybe you should go somewhere else." Darius tried not to grit his teeth.

Tetsu looked over at Adelaide and Kurt. Kurt looked at Darius then down at the ground. Adelaide kept her chin up and didn't avert her gaze.

"Whatever, I don't need this!" Tetsu turned and stomped off.

They stood in silence for a moment as Tetsu stalked across the playground. Adelaide sighed.

"I'm sorry if I overstepped," Darius said. He hadn't meant to lose his temper. The three of them turned and walked in the opposite direction. "I don't like bullies."

"It's okay," Adelaide said. Her face was impassive. "Tetsu is just, well, it's just his way. He'll be fine in a day or two."

Darius looked over at Kurt who looked doubtful.

"Did you guys see the article on the house with the Frankenstein monster?" Darius asked, changing the subject. "I was hoping for more answers. Like who owns the house, and where'd they get the bodies?"

"I did," Adelaide said. "There was almost nothing in the article."

"They can't publish the real story. Then people would ask even more questions," Kurt pointed out.

"So, what else is this town hiding?" Darius asked.

The three of them looked at each other, but before they could make any suggestions, the bell called them back inside.

***

The bus stopped at the corner of Pine Street. Adelaide, Tetsu, Kurt, and a handful of other kids filed off.

Adelaide turned and watched as Tetsu walked down the main road away from them.

"Guess it's just us," Kurt said as he and Adelaide walked up the road. The sky had turned a darker grey since lunchtime. Raindrops began to patter on the ground.

On most afternoons Sophie would grudgingly invite the lot of them to her house where they would hang out in the basement, which was lovingly referred to as the Hideout. Today Sophie had volleyball practice.

Whether they spent time in the Hideout or not, Tetsu always walked Adelaide home and then used her backyard to enter the forest. From there he cut back up onto his street. Today Tetsu walked the long way home along the road.

"Guess so." Adelaide gave Kurt a small but genuine smile.

The pair walked in a comfortable silence until they reached Kurt's house. Adelaide looked up at the sad beige bungalow the Zillman family called home. Kurt's dad's car was in the driveway.

"Did you want to come over?" Adelaide asked. "We could hang out in the backyard."

"Thanks, Adelaide." Kurt smiled at her. It was a tight smile and he looked toward the door with apprehension. "I appreciate it, but I should just get home."

"If you change your mind, you know where I am, okay?" Adelaide put her hand on Kurt's arm.

Kurt nodded, then turned and walked toward his front door.

No one on Pine Street liked Mr. Zillman. He was an angry man with a short temper. Adelaide often wondered if Mrs. Zillman even liked her husband. He was slightly overweight with a receding hairline and he spent most of his time passed out in their living room chair. He wasn't too bad most of the time, so long as he had a beer, but it was the other times you had to watch out for.

Adelaide looked on as Kurt gently opened the front door and stepped inside. He glanced back at her and she gave him her most encouraging smile. The front door closed and Adelaide continued on toward her house. She glanced at the houses on the street as she walked along. She liked to keep an eye on the yards and watch as plants grew and died back.

Adelaide climbed the rotting front steps of her

own house and crossed the porch to the front door. She glanced back at her mother's beat-up sedan and twisted the door handle. It opened and she stepped inside.

"Hey, baby! Is that you?" Belinda called from upstairs.

"Hi Mama." Adelaide slipped her shoes off and carried them and her backpack upstairs.

"You aren't spending time with your friends today?" Belinda stepped out of her room. She was dressed in an oversized T-shirt and a pair of underwear. Adelaide suspected Rico had stopped by for a lunch break, then been on his way again.

"No, not today. Sophie has volleyball," Adelaide replied in an even tone.

"All right, well you can always invite them over, baby." Belinda gave her a warm smile.

"Thanks, Mama. Everyone was busy today. I'm going to get my homework done." Adelaide gestured toward her room, which was across the hall from her mother's.

"Good luck! I know you'll knock 'em dead!" Belinda beamed at her.

Adelaide gave her a small smile as she opened the door to her own room and stepped inside. The walls were a faded pale pink. Like the rest of the house, the wooden floorboards were worn and dull. Her double bed was decorated with a few accent pillows and a pink and white floral bedspread. A small collection of stuffed animals nestled together at the foot of her bed. There was a bookshelf stuffed with used and worn copies of various novels, including *Connie, Playing with Fire, Deenie,* and several Nancy Drew mysteries. The window on the back wall looked out over the backyard and the forest beyond.

Adelaide could often see birds flitting from tree to tree and squirrels scampering this way and that. She looked out her window and noticed a large black crow perched on the fence. Its head swiveled as it let out an angry series of caws.

Adelaide frowned, set her backpack down on the sturdy wooden desk, and pulled out her school books. The crow cawed again as she ran her fingers along the spines of cassette cases on the shelf next to the desk.

***

Tetsu kicked a small stone and watched as it skipped along the pavement. He shoved his hands deeper into his khaki pockets as he walked up the street. A group of three kids walked just ahead of him. They kept glancing back at him, which caused Tetsu's scowl to deepen.

"Wonder what his problem is?" one boy muttered to his friend.

"Him and Adelaide are in some fight," the other boy replied.

Tetsu reached the stone and kicked it again. It skipped forward and almost hit the first boy.

"Uh-uh. I heard Adelaide and the new guy are a couple now," the sister said. "He's jealous."

"I can hear you!" Tetsu called out.

The trio exchanged a quick glance and hurried up their road toward their destinations, a pair of houses side-by-side.

Tetsu flipped them the bird as they looked back at him.

He carried on down the street toward his own house, which sat close to the forest's edge. Unlike Adelaide's house, most of the properties along the woods on Alder Street had been built with tall fences devoid of any gates. The forest floor dropped off suddenly and the properties here sat perched on the edge of a precipice.

Tetsu glanced toward the Horchuk house as he passed it. It was the closest one to Pine Street, and the only one with forest access. It was two doors down from Tetsu's. Normally, after he dropped Adelaide at her house, he would have cut through the forest and then through the Horchuk property to get home.

Tetsu kicked another rock and watched as it skipped down the street. His gaze shifted back to the Horchuk property as something in the large bushes moved. Tetsu paused and cocked his head to the side.

There was a long, low growl and the bush rustled.

Tetsu hesitated, then stepped closer.

The branches and leaves shook as a dark shape emerged. Light glinted off its eyes.

Tetsu turned and bolted toward his house.

The creature growled again, hot on his heels.

Tetsu risked a glance over his shoulder; the black mass was gaining on him. Tetsu winced as he stumbled over a small pothole. Pain shot up his ankle. He staggered forward, his chest pounding. He'd reached his driveway now. With one last push, he sprinted toward the front steps.

Tetsu opened the front door and slammed it closed behind him. He collapsed against it, his breath heaving.

Three

Darius sat down on the plush taupe rug in the main room of the pool house. The floor across the main level was off-white tile, but the rug was soft and comfortable. *My Aim is True* by Elvis Costello played quietly in the background while Darius worked through his math equations. His multiplication tables had been drilled into his head years prior and he jotted the answers into his workbook without too much difficulty. The album was two songs in when there was a brief knock at the door.

"Darius, dear?" Miranda called as she opened the door. "Are you in here?"

"Hi, Mom." Darius looked up and smiled.

"There you are." She smiled back. "What are you doing out here?"

"Homework. I like it out here." The pool house was one of Darius' favourite locations on the property and he hoped one day he could convince his parents to let him sleep in the guest bedrooms on the upper floor. He glanced around at the simple décor of the living room of the pool house. The main house, which had no shortage of dark, heavy wooden picture frames filled with Expressionist Art and uncomfortable furniture, felt too big. Darius didn't know a lot about interior design, but he wasn't as confident as his mother was that the interior designer she'd hired could make the large estate feel like home.

"Fair enough." Miranda smoothed the palms of her hands on her skirt and stepped over to the couch. Darius put down his pencil.

"Something I can help you with?" Darius asked.

"No, no." Miranda smoothed her skirt again as she sat down. She began to purse her lips, then stopped. She forced a small smile onto her face. "I wanted to check in and see how you are."

"I'm fine." Darius kept his tone light.

"Good. I'm glad. And everything is okay at school?" She held her smile for longer than she should have.

Darius felt unsettled.

"It's good, Mom." Darius forced a smile. He looked between her and his homework. This had to do with Boston, he was sure of it. He picked his pencil back up.

"I'm glad." She smiled again. "I'm always here if you want to talk."

Darius nodded. "Okay, got it. Just trying to get my homework done." He gestured with his pencil at the notebook and textbook laid out on the coffee table in front of him.

"And you aren't feeling,"—she paused for a moment, searching for the right word—"frustrated about anything? You're getting along with everyone?"

Darius sighed. His mother had been like this since the incident at his previous school. He had never meant for it to escalate as much as it did.

"I promise I'm fine. I'm getting along with everyone. I'm making lots of friends." Darius gave his most convincing smile. He wondered if this had to do with his outburst with Tetsu.

"Okay, all right." Miranda stood up and ran her palms against her skirt again. "If it changes, if anyone frustrates you, you know you can talk to me, right?"

"Thanks, Mom." Darius willed her to leave, and then remembered his conversation with Adelaide earlier that day. "Oh, I want to host a party. It could really help me make more friends. This Saturday, if that's okay with you."

Miranda's face softened into a genuine smile. "That sounds lovely!" Miranda beamed. Darius breathed a sigh of relief. "And your sister and her classmates will be able to come, too, of course?"

"Of course," Darius agreed. He'd suspected that would be the case and didn't want to push his luck.

"Well, then I hope you kids have fun. Just let us know what you need, all right?" Miranda kissed the top of Darius' head then walked to the door. She turned and studied him as she opened the door. "I love you, Darius."

"I love you, too, Mom."

Darius sighed and slumped back against the sofa as soon as the door closed. He wished more than anything his family could put Boston behind them.

***

Adelaide settled in at her desk and turned her attention to her homework. She was somewhat distracted by a list of songs for a mixtape forming in the back of her mind. Each time she thought of a song, she jotted it down on a piece of lined paper.

Adelaide worked through her math assignment. Her stomach rumbled as she closed her textbook. As if on cue, there was a small knock and the door to Adelaide's room opened. Her mother poked her head inside.

"So, I was thinking grilled cheese sandwiches for dinner." Belinda smiled. "I can start them now. What do you think?"

Adelaide looked at the list of songs she had compiled and set her pencil down. "Sounds good. Why don't I keep you company?"

"Oh, you don't have to, baby! I can putter away all by myself," Belinda assured her in her bubbly voice.

"I want to," Adelaide insisted. On rare occasions Belinda had the urge to cook and on these occasions the house smelled like burnt: burnt toast, burnt soup, burnt grilled cheese sandwiches, burnt frozen pizza, or burnt eggs. Always burnt. "Why don't I put on the music?"

"Oooh, yes! I love when you pick the music," Belinda praised.

"Thanks, Mama." Adelaide gathered up her song list and followed her mother downstairs. "I'll be there in a second, Mama." She stopped in the living room, crouched down and flipped through her mother's record collection. Adelaide pulled out *She's so Unusual* by Cyndi Lauper, set it to play and turned it up.

Adelaide walked into the kitchen and nodded at the volume of the music. It was perfect, unlike the state of the kitchen. Breadcrumbs were scattered across the dark green countertop next to the toaster. Several coffee mugs, two plates and a bowl were in the sink. The floor was a mess of food debris.

"I love this one, great choice." Belinda beamed at her. She had already buttered slices of white bread.

Adelaide smiled as her mother took a jar of Jalapeño Tex-Mex Cheez Whiz out of the fridge and smeared liberal amounts of it across the slices of the bread. "Thanks, Mama." Adelaide glanced at the garbage bin, which had almost overflowed. A bread bag with the bread ends still inside protruded like a tongue taunting her. "You don't have to throw out the ends you know." Adelaide set her pencil and list of song ideas down on the banquet-style table and walked to the garbage can where she wrestled the garbage bag free. She didn't love bread ends, or the bread bum as Sophie called it, but they were perfectly fine and far better than an empty cupboard.

"The ends are terrible!" Belinda remarked. She glanced over. "You don't have to do that."

"It's okay, Mama, I've got it." Adelaide folded the top of the bag over, squished the garbage down into the bag and tied the whole thing closed. She eyed her mother's progress, but decided to chance it.

Adelaide slipped a pair of shoes she kept by the

back door onto her feet and carried the bag out the back. She walked across the wooden deck, down the side stairs, and around to the dented silver garbage bin on the side of the house.

Somewhere toward the back of the property, a bird cawed. Adelaide hefted the bag into the can and resecured the lid with a slight clang as the metal reverberated against itself. She wondered how many of Madonna's songs she should include on the party cassette. Madonna was good to dance to and Sophie loved her. She was halfway up the steps lost in thought about if she could fit "Material Girl," "Like a Virgin" and this summer's hit, "Papa Don't Preach," on the cassette when she noticed something move out of the corner of her eye.

There was another loud caw as a big black crow swooped straight toward her.

Four

The crow shot toward Adelaide. Its beady little eyes stared at her as it closed the gap between them. Adelaide stood, frozen on the spot. At the last second, she dropped down and banged her knees on the wooden steps. The bird slammed into the house with a sickening thud.

Adelaide took several short breaths and looked around. The crow lay in an unmoving heap next to her. The air was still. She took a deep breath and forced herself to stand. Her knee hurt, but she hadn't ripped her pants.

She leaned over the bird, curious what had driven it to attack her. She wondered if it had been hungry and suddenly remembered her mother, unsupervised in the kitchen.

Adelaide scurried up the steps and back into the house. The sandwiches were in the pan on the stove. She looked at the dial, which was set to a medium temperature, and washed her hands at the sink.

"So, what were you working on upstairs?" Belinda asked, her tone playful. Adelaide imagined the music from the living room had drowned out the bird thumping into the house.

Adelaide glanced at her list of songs on the table and answered in her usual monotone. "Mixed tape for a party. I still have to record it, but I was going over the order of the songs." She glanced back at the window and wondered if there were any more crows loitering.

"That sounds fun! Is Blondie on there? The Beach Boys? The Beatles? Tell me there's some Pat Benatar."

"All of the above, yes," Adelaide assured her as she broke her gaze from the window. Adelaide credited her own love of music to her mother's, as well as some of the previous roommates.

"You rock at this music stuff, baby." Belinda turned to face Adelaide. "So, will we host it?"

"The party? No, Mama. Darius will host it. I mean, we're co-hosts, but he has a pool, so…" Adelaide trailed off.

"Oh," Belinda said. She turned back to the stove. "That's too bad. It would be pretty fun if we hosted a party, wouldn't it, baby? We could buy chips. And soda!"

"Mmmhmm." Adelaide thought of how empty the pantry had been this morning. "Next time. How's the job hunt?"

"Good! It's good. I dropped off a bunch of résumés today, actually." Belinda turned and beamed at Adelaide.

"Good job." Adelaide smiled. Between the groceries and the résumés, her mother had accomplished more than Adelaide had anticipated.

"Thank you," Belinda said as she turned back the stove. She used a spatula to look under the sandwich and see how toasted it was. Adelaide cringed as Belinda turned the element up higher. "Oh, I picked something up for you today! Hang on, I'll go get it." Belinda abandoned the stove and walked out of the kitchen.

Adelaide scampered to the stove, turned down the element and waited. She listened to the footfalls and knew her mother had gone upstairs. She waited another moment, then checked the sandwiches and flipped them. They were perfectly golden.

Adelaide sat back up at the table as her mother sauntered in with her hands behind her back.

"Ta-da!" Belinda announced with a flourish as she produced a set of earrings. They were black and white lightning bolts. "I thought they'd match your wrist cuff!"

Adelaide smiled. "I love them. Thank you." Adelaide was never without her wrist cuff. The band of leather decorated with squares of white and black metal felt like a shield on her wrist. She'd found it under the couch one day. None of their roommates at the time had claimed ownership of it, and no one else ever stepped forward to claim it. It had been on her wrist ever since.

"Oh, they're perfect!" Belinda smiled at the sandwiches on the stove. "I don't even remember flipping them."

"They smell great," Adelaide offered. She glanced out the window toward the woods.

Belinda lifted the sandwiches and looked under them. "Not quite ready yet. So, what will you wear to the party?"

"Jeans?" Adelaide shrugged. "A shirt of some kind?"

Belinda surveyed her daughter and shook her head ever so slightly She checked the sandwiches again, and moved them to their plates where she cut them into quarters. Belinda turned the element off, picked up the plates and carried them to the table, then sat in the wooden chair opposite Adelaide.

"For you, baby," Belinda said as she put the plates on the table. "We should go shopping tomorrow morning."

"Shopping?" Adelaide glanced toward the cupboards and thought of her mother's lack of employment.

"Shopping. That thing where you go to a store and buy things." Belinda teased. "We'll pick you up something for this party."

"Okay," Adelaide hesitated.

"That smells good," Violet said as she entered the room. She was in her early twenties and had been living with them as a roommate for almost six months. Her short brown hair was a mess and she wore sweatpants and an oversized T-shirt that read, "Frankie Says Relax." Violet's eyes were ringed with red but were less puffy than usual today. Adelaide always wondered what could be so terrible a person needed to cry as much as Violet did.

"I can make you a sandwich," Belinda offered.

"You made them?" Violet asked. She looked between Belinda and Adelaide.

"I did," Belinda beamed. She took a bite of her grilled cheese and got up from the table. "Sit down, Violet."

Violet hesitated, but did as she was told.

Belinda prepared the sandwich and placed it in the pan, which she turned up to maximum. Violet looked at Adelaide. Adelaide avoided her gaze. "She Bop" came onto the stereo.

"Oh, I love this one! I'm going to turn it up!"

Belinda danced her way out of the room.

Violet looked between Adelaide and the stove. Adelaide looked at the table, then she sighed and stood.

"I knew it," Violet gloated.

"She was so proud," Adelaide explained. She strode to the stove and turned the element down. The volume of the music increased and Adelaide could hear her mother's tone-deaf voice belt out the words alongside Cyndi Lauper. Adelaide walked back to the table and took another bite of her sandwich.

"She shouldn't be cooking," Violet pointed out. "She makes the house stink every time she does. And she ruined that pot."

Adelaide recalled the pot. She had scrubbed it for a solid thirty minutes after her mother thought it was a good idea to make custard.

"Listen to how happy she is." Adelaide gestured to the room. She took another bite of her sandwich.

"I heard from my mom," Violet said, changing the subject.

"How was that?" Adelaide asked. Violet often locked herself in her room for hours after a call from her mother. When she emerged, she insisted she was fine. Adelaide, who always noticed her puffy eyes, would just nod and squeeze her arm.

"She says she was attacked by birds. So that was something." Violet almost smiled.

"Really? Is she okay?" Adelaide thought of the crow outside. She wondered if the two incidents were connected to Grover Jergen. Violet's mother lived in the Seattle area, but Adelaide wasn't certain exactly where.

"She told me I'd never amount to anything, so she's as fine as ever." Violet sighed.

"I'm sorry, Violet." Adelaide walked back to the stove and checked the sandwich. "Mama!" she called. "You might need to flip it!" She sat back down at the table and squeezed Violet's hand.

"Right!" Belinda bounded back into the room. "I almost got distracted." She picked up the spatula and flipped the sandwich over. "Look at that! Perfect again!"

***

"Heartbreak Hotel" could just be heard over the low hum of chatter in The Diner, a popular and inexpensive eatery. The restaurant was half full. Groups of teenagers sipped milkshakes and shared plates of fries. Parents fussed over their children while they ate a family meal. A grey-haired couple nursed their cups of coffee. A pair of middle-aged men dressed in slacks and sport jackets sat at one of the booths that looked out in the parking lot.

"This tastes like shit," Gary Stevens said as he took a sip of his coffee.

"I'm sure the waitress is doing the best she can," Ray Gregory said. He was about an inch shorter than Gary with a paunchy belly and a softer face. "Where do you want to look for this guy?"

"This town is shit." Gary took another sip of his coffee and looked out the window.

"That's why we're here. To clean it up." Ray tipped a few photos out of the large manilla envelope and flipped through them. "What do you think of this Jergen guy?"

"It doesn't matter what I think. It matters what I know." Gary nodded toward the file on the table, took another sip of his coffee and grimaced at the taste. "The man disappeared from his job and took off with his research. He's experimenting on birds and making them go bat shit."

"Maybe we can just talk to him. No harm, no fowl?" Ray cracked a hopeful smile.

Gary raised an eyebrow and looked at him over the rim of his coffee cup. "Shit is shit, Ray."

Five

Darius tapped his foot impatiently in the backseat of the Lincoln Town Car. He glanced at the clock on the dashboard. They were late.

The quiet murmur of a news broadcaster on the radio did little to ease the palpable tension in the car.

The side of his father's cheek rippled as he clenched his jaw. His knuckles were pale as he gripped the steering wheel. It was no secret that Drew Belcouer hated being late.

Davia fidgeted in the front seat.

"Sit still," Drew barked.

Davia folded her hands and kept quiet.

Drew pulled the car up to the curb in front of the school. A small trickle of students made their way into the building, but the grounds were otherwise empty. The bell had already rung.

Darius grabbed his bag, unbuckled his seatbelt and opened the car door. "Thanks, Dad," he said as he scampered out of the car. He'd only just closed the car door when Drew pulled away from the curb.

"I hate when he's like that," Davia complained.

"You don't do much to help it," Darius pointed out. Davia had been late to breakfast again this morning.

"What does that mean?" Davia asked.

"Never mind, Davia. We should get to class before we have to check in at the office."

Darius hurried through the front doors of the school. The cloakroom was empty as he hung his bag up and made his way to his seat. He grinned at Adelaide. He wasn't sure if it was his imagination, but she looked relieved to see him.

***

Adelaide breathed an inward sigh of relief as Darius took his seat next to her. She couldn't stop thinking about the bird outside her house. "I have to talk to you." Her voice was quiet and she glanced toward Mr. McKenzie. "Recess." She turned her attention back to the front of the classroom as Mr. McKenzie began to take attendance.

Adelaide looked out the large bank of windows. Small raindrops fell from the grey sky. The nearby tree branches swayed slightly in the breeze. A single crow circled through the sky and landed on a nearby branch.

Adelaide shuddered.

"Adelaide Winter?" Mr. McKenzie called.

"Here," Adelaide replied. She raised her hand and smiled at her teacher. He smiled back.

Mr. McKenzie had just finished rollcall when the PA system came to life.

"Would Tetsu Nomura please report to the office. Tetsu Nomura to the office immediately."

Tetsu scowled at the speaker as though it, not a person in the office, were responsible for his summons.

"Go ahead, Tetsu," Mr. McKenzie said.

Tetsu stood and walked out of the classroom.

"Wonder what that's about?" Kurt asked.

"No idea," Adelaide answered. He'd been even more subdued this morning. Adelaide desperately wanted their fight to be over, but she wanted Tetsu to apologize and mean it. His words still stung.

Adelaide craned her neck as Tetsu left the room. Adelaide hoped he would give her a sign he was okay, but he just strode into the hallway. She fretted over his prolonged absence and struggled to pay attention to her studies. There was still no sign of him when the recess bell rang some time later.

"I'm a bit worried." Adelaide admitted as she pulled on her coat.

"I'm sure he's fine," Darius assured her.

"No, this is unusual," Adelaide insisted as they exited the building.

"Maybe he came outside but he's avoiding you because he doesn't want to apologize."

"Maybe." Adelaide studied him and wondered how much he knew.

"Oh!" Darius said as he ran his fingers through his hair. He smiled at Adelaide. "My parents are totally fine with the party. We can invite people today, if you still want to do this."

"That's awesome." Adelaide breathed a small sigh of relief. "Thank you, Darius. I'm happy to co-host with you. I've already started a mixed tape."

"Really?" Darius asked. "That's rad! I hate when people think you can just put an album on."

Adelaide gave Darius a half smile and nodded. "Exactly." Adelaide had a nagging feeling she had something to tell Darius, but she was too worried about Tetsu to remember what it was.

Recess finished and everyone filed back into their classrooms. Tetsu's backpack still hung in the cloakroom.

41

The morning wore on, but there was no sign of Tetsu. Mr. McKenzie gave Adelaide a sympathetic smile as her gaze alternated between the clock and the door. After the lunch bell rang, Adelaide picked at her peanut butter and jam sandwich. Both Kurt and Darius gave up trying to make conversation with her. At the sound of the second bell, which denoted they were allowed outside, Adelaide collected Tetsu's lunch bag from his backpack and walked by the office.

Tetsu sat just inside the office door on one of the uncomfortable plastic chairs often reserved for sick children whose parents hadn't picked them up yet. His head was hung and he looked deflated. It was a depressing sight given his usual confidence.

"Hey," Adelaide said as she sat down next to him.

He looked up. "What are you doing here?"

"Excuse me, you can't be speaking with him," Shirley, the receptionist, interjected.

"Pardon me?" Adelaide asked in her monotone voice. She looked up at the woman behind the desk. Shirley had worked at the school as long as Adelaide could remember. She was a sour-faced woman whose hair always looked like it had been pulled too-tight into a bun.

"You can't be speaking with him. Run along."

Shirley waved her hand toward the door.

"You're telling me," Adelaide clarified, "that even though I'm a student in this school, I'm not allowed in the office?" She held Shirley's gaze.

"Are you sick?" Shirley asked in a challenging tone. "Did you need me to call your mother?"

"Why is he here?" Adelaide gestured at Tetsu. "Is he sick? Did you call his mother?" Adelaide's tone was impassive, but her frustration was growing.

"He's in trouble." Shirley's nostrils flared.

"What did you do?" Adelaide looked at Tetsu.

Tetsu shrugged.

Adelaide turned back to the front desk. "What did he do?"

"I don't have to answer your questions, Adelaide." Shirley put her hands on her hips.

Adelaide took a deep breath. She knew an argument with a grownup was almost always pointless. They didn't listen. She wanted to yell or to scream, but she knew she'd be told to calm down. She hated when people told her to calm down.

"Has Tetsu's mother been called?" Adelaide asked. Her voice remained even.

"Yes. She didn't answer. Now why don't you—"

"Is your mother supposed to be out today?" Adelaide asked as she turned back to Tetsu.

He shook his head. He looked defeated, a shell of the person she knew.

Adelaide stood and turned back to the reception desk. Her voice was firm now. Her frustration roiled in her stomach like a kettle about to boil. "When was the last time you tried her?"

"I don't think that's any of your—"

"It actually is. He's my friend. You've held him in the office like a criminal for the last several hours." Adelaide forced her voice to remain even as she spoke. She held Tetsu's lunch bag up. "He hasn't even been allowed to go get his lunch." She handed it to Tetsu in an exaggerated fashion. "So, if you'll excuse me, I'll spend my lunch in the school office, with my friend. If you have a problem with it, I suppose you can call my mother." Adelaide sat back down in the seat next to Tetsu.

Shirley sighed. "If I call his mother, will you leave?"

"Yes. As soon as you get a hold of her. Or the bell goes." Adelaide watched as Shirley picked up the phone and plugged in a few numbers.

"Hello? Mrs. Nomura? This is Shirley from James Morrison Elementary School." Shirley looked over at

Adelaide and indicated she should leave.

Adelaide stood and squeezed Tetsu's shoulder. "If you didn't do whatever they accused you of, your mom will back you up."

Tetsu nodded, but continued to look dejected.

"No, he's in trouble." Shirley explained into the receiver. "I need you to come down to the school. I don't think we should discuss it over the phone."

Adelaide glanced back into the office as she stepped into the hall. Shirley winced and moved the phone away from her ear. Mrs. Nomura did not like bad news. Adelaide was confident she would give Shirley an earful. Adelaide smiled in satisfaction as she imagined what Mrs. Nomura would say when she learned how long Tetsu had been in the office. She exited the school and found Darius and Kurt just outside the doors.

"Everything okay?" Darius asked.

"Not really. They won't tell me what he did." Adelaide frowned.

"He didn't tell you?" Darius asked.

Adelaide shook her head.

"I heard Mrs. Anders' car was keyed," Kurt offered. "That's your sister's teacher right?"

Darius nodded.

"Oh, that would do it." Adelaide gave a single nod. Mrs. Anders always seemed to have it out for Tetsu. If there was damage to her car, Mrs. Anders would be convinced Tetsu had something to do with it.

"Did Tetsu do it?" Darius asked.

"I doubt it," Adelaide answered.

"Maybe," Kurt said.

"Kurt, he wouldn't do that," Adelaide said. "For one thing, he'd be scared his mother would find out. For another, when would he have done it?"

"That's a good point," Kurt relented.

"He's scared of his mother?" Darius asked.

"You'll see," Adelaide answered. "Shirley called her."

Darius looked intrigued. Kurt looked like he had sucked on a lemon.

Mrs. Nomura arrived less than ten minutes later. She was a slight woman with an angular face and dark eyes. Her skin was smooth and flawless. Mrs. Nomura surveyed everything, as though danger lurked around the corner. When she spoke, she spoke in broken English. Adelaide had long suspected Mrs. Nomura did this not because she couldn't speak English in full sentences, but because she didn't care enough about the people she spoke with to give them more of her time than she needed to.

46

It took her seconds to spot Adelaide and she strode toward her.

"Adelaide. What Tetsu do?" Mrs. Nomura barked.

"Hello, Mrs. Nomura. I don't know exactly. I heard a car was keyed, but I don't think he did it. He's in the office."

Mrs. Nomura narrowed her eyes and studied Adelaide. Adelaide felt as though Mrs. Nomura gazed into her very soul in search of the truth. She looked over at Kurt and then Darius.

"Kurtis." Mrs. Nomura gave a single brisk nod. "I not know you," she said as she narrowed her eyes at Darius.

"I'm Darius Belcouer. I'm new this year. It's a pleasure to meet you." Darius smiled at her.

Mrs. Nomura continued to stare at Darius for a moment. Her face was impassive, but she didn't break eye contact. Darius tried to hold her gaze, then gave a small nod and looked at the ground. Mrs. Nomura turned back to Adelaide and nodded toward the door. "You show me."

Adelaide moved ahead of her and opened it. She nodded goodbye to Darius and Kurt as she held the door open for Mrs. Nomura. The pair walked to the office. Shirley noticed Adelaide first and opened her mouth, but

Mrs. Nomura spoke first.

"Why my son not in class? Where is principal-san? I drive all the way here. He should be ready."

Shirley's eyes widened and she skuttled to the principal's door.

Mrs. Nomura turned to Tetsu and spoke quickly in Japanese. Then she turned to Adelaide. "Thank you, Adelaide. I take it from here." Mrs. Nomura nodded slightly.

"Yes, Mrs. Nomura." Adelaide stole one last look at Tetsu before she left the office. His head wasn't hung quite as low, but his gaze was still on the floor.

***

"That's Tetsu's mom?" Darius asked Kurt. He still felt unsettled by the way Mrs. Nomura's eyes had studied him. He felt like she saw every one of his flaws.

"That's Tetsu's mom," Kurt confirmed.

"Wow. I mean, my dad looks strict, but ..." Darius trailed off as he looked at the school doors.

"You don't want to be on Mrs. Nomura's bad side." Kurt gave a slight shake of his head.

"Is he going to be okay?" Darius asked. He

48

remembered when his father had been called to the office at his old school. He felt a pang of sympathy for Tetsu.

"Who can say?" Kurt grimaced.

The two stood in silence. Groups of students walked past the doors and most of them ignored Kurt. A few girls looked over and smiled at Darius. One of them giggled as she passed by. Darius thought he should invite them to the party, but he worried they would get the wrong idea.

"No, I'm telling you, he was attacked," a girl in a baby blue outfit said.

"I heard you, he was attacked by a dog," her friend replied.

"No, my sister's boyfriend was attacked by a vicious dog-like-thing," the girl in blue insisted.

Darius' ears prickled. He wondered if there was a mystery they could look into closer to home.

"A dog," the second girl repeated as she rolled her eyes.

Darius didn't recognize them from his class and suspected they were a year younger than him. He started to walk toward them. The bell rang. Darius cast a glance at the girls as they rounded the corner of the building toward the side doors.

"Come on, Darius. We should get back," Kurt said.

"Adelaide will meet us there."

Darius sighed and followed Kurt back into the halls. His spirits lifted slightly as he remembered the party he and Adelaide needed to invite people to.

Six

The school day had come to a close. Adelaide had ridden home on the bus with Kurt and the two of them stood outside his house. Gus Zillman's car wasn't in the driveway.

"You're going to check on Tetsu, aren't you?" Kurt asked.

Adelaide nodded.

"Are you still mad at him?" he asked.

"Yes," Adelaide said flatly.

"You're a good friend, Adelaide." Kurt smiled at her.

"Did you want to come?" Adelaide asked. She already knew what his answer would be.

Kurt glanced back at his house and shook his head. "I should be here in case my dad gets home early. Besides, his mom scares me."

The corners of Adelaide's mouth turned up into a small smile. "I'll see you tomorrow, Kurt."

"Tomorrow." Kurt agreed. "Good luck," he added as he turned and walked up the front steps of his house.

Adelaide carried on down Pine Street.

There was a single truck parked outside her house. It was a beat-up old pickup that belonged to their roommate Waylon.

Adelaide climbed the rickety front steps, unlocked the front door and tucked her backpack inside. She knew Waylon would be sleeping off his nightshift. She doubted her presence would wake him, but she hadn't been able to stop thinking about Tetsu. Even after his mother had arrived at the school, Tetsu hadn't returned to class.

The house was still. Adelaide was sure no one else was home. She liked it when the house was still. Adelaide stepped back out onto the front porch, pulled the door closed and locked it. An old wooden fence separated the side yard from the front and Adelaide lifted the latch on the gate and stepped through. She walked along the side of the house to the backyard. It was a large yard, bigger than most on her street.

The lawn was uneven and unkempt. There was a large worn shed not too far from the house, but most of the yard was just an open expanse. A handful of young pine trees grew close to the fence line. Fallen pine needles and broken branches littered the ground around them.

Adelaide punched the four-digit code into the

push-button keypad and turned the handle. Her mother had been resistant to getting the keypad installed, but Jezikiah, a former roommate, had pushed for it. He'd pointed out how just about anybody could walk onto the property from the woods or cut through their yard from the street. In the end, Belinda had agreed. Adelaide often wondered if Jezikiah had just convinced her simply by offering to pay for it.

Adelaide swung the wooden gate open and stepped out into the forest. The gate closed behind her. She made her way along the narrow trail toward Alder Street. Adelaide slipped through the wooden gate on the edge of the Horchuk property and glanced toward the house.

Mrs. Horchuk moved back and forth in front of the window. She held a small bundle in her arms, and she jiggled it as she moved.

Adelaide gave a small wave. She thought she saw Mrs. Horchuk nod back. Life hadn't seemed easier for Tetsu's neighbour since the baby had arrived. Any time Adelaide passed by Mrs. Horchuk seemed to have her hands full. Adelaide had a hard time imagining her own mother carrying her around that much. She'd asked her about it once. Belinda had just said she was a quiet baby.

Adelaide made her way across the street to the

Nomura house.

It was a two-storey building from the front, but there was a partial basement that wasn't visible from the road. The lawn was a luscious green and without a weed in sight. A colourful array of roses lined both sides of the driveway and the front of the house. Mrs. Nomura's rose garden was as meticulous as the lawn, and Adelaide knew she was proud of it.

Adelaide paused at a yellow rose that had recently bloomed. She couldn't help but lean in and smell it. She took in a deep breath and savoured the sweet smell. She sighed as she exhaled. Adelaide turned back to the house and made her way to the door. She knocked and tried not to hold her breath.

Mrs. Nomura opened the door. She pursed her lips and appraised Adelaide. Then she held the door open and indicated for Adelaide to enter. "You come in. Tetsu in his room."

Adelaide bowed her head. "Thank you, Mrs. Nomura." She took off her shoes in the entryway and set them neatly on the mat by the front door. She ignored the guest slippers and pulled on her own, a gift from Mrs. Nomura that always sat waiting for her.

The décor in Tetsu's house was beautiful but sparse.

A meticulously cared for bonsai sat atop a perfectly polished side table in the entryway. A set of matching hangings lined the hallway wall. The low table in the dinning room was always free of clutter and the carpet in the house always appeared to be freshly vacuumed.

Adelaide walked up the stairs and her hand trailed along the smooth banister. At the top of the stairs was a small table with a select array of family photos, all in coordinated frames. She paused to admire the photos. Tetsu wore a solemn expression and perfectly pressed clothes in each picture.

Adelaide rapped on Tetsu's bedroom door. Tetsu opened it a moment later.

"Oh, hey," Tetsu said. He looked surprised to see her.

Adelaide tilted her head to the side and studied him.

The two of them stared at each other for a moment.

"Did you want to …" Tetsu inclined his head and indicated she could enter the room.

"Sure," Adelaide said. Her voice wasn't quite her usual even tone, but she didn't exaggerate it either. She stepped into Tetsu's room, which was just as meticulous as the rest of the house. The top of his desk was bare, all of the writing implements stored neatly in containers inside the drawers. His bed was carefully made. Not a single poster adorned his wall, though a wood-block print depicting a samurai was hung above his headboard. "Is everything okay? What happened?"

"That?" Tetsu smirked. "Oh, they didn't see my mom coming."

"Are you in trouble?" Adelaide asked. Mrs. Nomura had seemed as though she was in a good mood, but it was hard to tell.

"Naw. She yelled at them a whole bunch for making me miss classes when they didn't have proof I did anything. Then, get this," Tetsu laughed, "she tells me we're leaving because they wasted enough of our time and she drives me to The Diner. The Diner!"

"No!" Adelaide gasped.

"Oh yeah! And she ordered us both burgers and fries." Tetsu plunked down on his desk chair.

"Both of you?" Adelaide's eyes widened.

"Both of us. She ate all of hers. Then she pays up and we drive home. Not a word about the school."

"Not one?" Adelaide furrowed her brow.

"Yep. So, I've just been kickin' it in my room. I don't think I'm in trouble. I'm just reading comics and waiting to see what she does next."

"Huh." Adelaide plopped down on Tetsu's bed. "Maybe she actually feels bad you got in trouble for something you didn't do?"

"I guess. I like it." Tetsu grinned.

"It was about Mrs. Anders' car, right? Do we know who did it?"

"It was. And not a clue, but I'd like to shake their hand. Those were some harsh words on that witch's car." Tetsu chuckled.

Adelaide frowned. Mrs. Anders was her least favourite teacher at the school, but she didn't think she deserved to be called names or have her vehicle damaged. She was glad, at least, that Tetsu had selected a "w" instead of another letter.

"Come on, you know she's always had it out for me. She just got what she deserved!" Tetsu grinned, then his face clouded over. He stood and walked to the window where he looked out at the street below. "I'm really sorry, you know. Really. I shouldn't have said it," Tetsu mumbled.

"What's that?" Adelaide asked in an exaggerated and perky tone. She pressed her lips together and raised her eyebrows.

"You're going to make me do this, aren't you?" Tetsu heaved a sigh. "Fine. I'm sorry." He turned and looked at her. "I was a jerk to you and you were still there for me."

A wave of relief flooded through Adelaide. Her face turned impassive and she dropped her voice to its usual even tone. "It was the meanest thing you've ever said to me, Tetsu Nomura. And I'm still mad about it. But I'll stop speaking that way now because I want to."

"Are we good?" Tetsu asked. Worry still clouded his face.

"No." Adelaide knew she needed more time. She stood and moved toward the door. "But we will be." Adelaide paused at the doorway. "There's a party Saturday at Darius' house. We invited both grade seven classes. You should come. We'll have pizza. And soda."

Tetsu could never resist pizza. Or soda.

***

Darius sat on the floor of the pool house and combed through the newspaper. He'd already read it twice, but he hoped to find some mention of a dog or bird attack. He ran his fingers through his hair.

"Is this what you do in here?" Davia scoffed.

Darius almost jumped. He had been so intent on the paper he hadn't heard the door open.

"What?" He looked up confused.

"Is this what you do in here?" she asked again. "You sit around and read newspapers like Dad? Boring!" Davia picked up the remote control from the coffee table and flopped on the couch.

"Davia, can you not—"

Images danced across the screen. Davia pressed another button and the sound of the television grew louder.

"Davia, come on." Darius sighed. "I was here first."

"Mom has that woman over again. I don't want to hear another word about Venetian blinds." Davia slipped her feet out of her shoes. She wiggled her socked feet as the footwear dropped onto the floor next to Darius.

"Really?" Darius gestured.

"What?" Davia shrugged. "So, big news about the party. You and Adelaide looked adorable as you announced the invitation to my class. Have you kissed her yet? Touched her boobs?"

"Grow up, Davia." Darius looked at the paper, then back up at his sister. "Hey, did you hear anything about a dog attack?"

"No." Davia used the remote to flick through the channels.

"Nothing?" Darius asked. He knew Davia liked to talk to people. She had been big into gossip at Wiltshire Preparatory Academy, he was sure of it. "I heard some girls at school mention one."

Davia looked away from the screen and held Darius' gaze. "Some girl? Two-timing Adelaide already." She shook her head. "I thought she'd be the one to cheat on you."

Darius sighed and looked back at the paper. Sometimes he wished he were an only child.

Seven

When the lunch bell rang on Friday, Darius fell in step with Adelaide. Kurt and Tetsu joined them. Adelaide began to walk the perimeter of the school grounds and the trio of boys followed.

Darius was both relieved and disappointed Adelaide and Tetsu had made amends. He could see Tetsu's friendship meant something to Adelaide, but all Darius could see was a loud-mouth rival for her attention.

"How'd it go with your mom yesterday?" Darius asked. If Tetsu was important to Adelaide he knew he had to make an effort.

"Fine. Why?" Tetsu eyed him with suspicion.

"No reason. I saw her arrive. She looks strict."

Tetsu scowled. "What do you know about it?"

"I just meant, I know it can be tough when your parents are strict," Darius offered.

"Sure, you do. I bet your parents are too busy at the country club to have any idea what you and the princess are up to," Tetsu spat.

Darius forced himself to take a breath. He wasn't sure where he'd gone wrong. Unless it was just trying to talk to Tetsu in the first place.

"Does anyone have a song request for the party?" Adelaide asked as she put her hand on Tetsu's arm. Darius sensed the tension dissipate. He took a deep breath.

"Oh," Kurt said. "How about that one you put on at Sophie's that time? 'Sunshine of Your Love.' That's what it's called, isn't it?"

"Consider it done, Kurt. Anyone else?" Adelaide asked.

"You've already put 'Take On Me' on there, right?" Tetsu asked.

Adelaide nodded. "I wouldn't forget your favourite song."

Darius tried to hide his surprise. He thought Tetsu would have more adventurous taste in music, especially being friends with Adelaide. He was curious to hear the completed cassette. "Maybe some Huey Lewis and the News? But I'm sure whatever you've got on there will be great," Darius said.

"Are you now?" Adelaide asked. Her voice was monotone, but Darius got the sense she was teasing him.

"Yes." He grinned at her.

Their walk had led the four of them near the playground where several groups of students congregated. Sophie branched off from Julie and some of the other girls and moved in their direction. She ignored the others and approached Darius.

"Did you want to come over to my house sometime?" Sophie asked. She played with a strand of her long blond hair.

"I'd love to," Tetsu said with an impish grin.

"Not you." Sophie scowled at Tetsu. She turned back to Darius and smiled. "Darius, did you want to come over? My mom could make us snacks and we could hang out. Just you and me."

"Oh, thanks Sophie," Darius said. "But maybe we should keep it as a group thing. I'd hate for people to not feel included."

"I, ah, um," Sophie stuttered. She looked between Darius and the others. "Fine, sure." Sophie recovered and smiled. "If that's what you want." She flicked her long blond hair over her shoulder and sauntered back toward Julie and her other friends.

"Well, gosh," Tetsu said with a smirk. "An invite from Sophie Katillion herself and you declined it. Her mom makes the best after school snacks."

Darius looked around to see if he'd misstepped. Kurt gazed out toward the playground at Farrah. Adelaide's solemn face was inscrutable.

***

The school day had drawn to a close and the friends of Pine Street had gathered in Sophie's basement in the Hideout. Adelaide sat in her usual spot on the floor near the record player. She flipped through the albums, all of whose covers she knew by heart. Tetsu reclined in the bean bag chair while Sophie sprawled across the couch. Kurt sat in the armchair with a textbook and his school binder.

Adelaide traced her fingers over the black dog on the cover of a Jethro Tull album and wondered what it would be like to camp with her friends in the wood when they got a bit older. She slid the album back into place and carried on, knowing her friends wouldn't enjoy Jethro Tull's music as much as she might.

"So, is Brody going to make out with you at the party?" Sophie asked. Her tone was light, but she smiled like a shark.

"What?" Adelaide turned and looked at Sophie.

"Come on, he has a huge crush on you. You two would look cute together." Sophie cooed. She stacked a piece of cheese onto a cracker and took a bite.

"Grody, Brody!" Tetsu laughed.

"I heard his notebook has hearts with your name in them," Sophie teased.

"Brody is fine,"—Adelaide frowned—"but I'm not interested in him like that."

"Is he coming to the party?" Kurt asked as he looked up from his homework.

"Yes. He wasn't sure, but Darius told him about the arcade machine in the pool house and he said he'd be there." Adelaide looked back down at the cover of *Dreamboat Annie* by Heart.

"What?" Tetsu wheeled. "He has an *arcade machine* in his *pool house?*"

"Sounds like." Adelaide shrugged. Her stomach rumbled and she hoped the noise was drowned out by the "Last Train to Clarksville" by The Monkees. She reached over to the table, placed a slice of cheese onto a cracker and took a bite.

"Well, you guys should probably get going," Sophie said. She looked at the plate of cheese and crackers and then picked it up. "It's almost dinner time. I'm sure your parents will want you home."

"Okay," Kurt said. He closed his book and slid it into his backpack.

Adelaide ate the last bite of her cracker and cheese and dusted her hands on her jeans. She picked up the album she had out and placed it back onto the shelf.

"It's early still," Tetsu argued. He looked longingly at the plate of cheese and crackers.

Adelaide lifted the needle off the turntable and slid *The Monkees* back into its cover. She placed the album back on the shelf and picked up her bag.

"My parents don't want people here too late tonight," Sophie said as she shepherded everyone out of the Hideout.

"Your parents don't care," Tetsu scoffed.

"Tetsu," Sophie warned as they filed out of the room onto the lower landing. She ushered everyone up the steps.

As she reached the landing at the front door, Adelaide glanced up the stairs.

"Are you all leaving already?" Sheila called as she stepped out from the kitchen.

"Yes, Mom. They all have to get home," Sophie replied as she opened the front door. "Bye, guys."

"Adelaide, sweetie, you are welcome to stay for dinner." Sheila smiled.

Adelaide could feel Sophie's gaze on her. She hoped Andy would come around the corner from his bedroom and wave goodbye.

"I'm okay, Mrs. Katillion. My mom needs me home," Adelaide lied. "And I've got a mixed tape to make for the party. Thank you, though. Really."

"If you're sure," Sheila said. She looked between Sophie and Adelaide.

"She's sure," Sophie said with a smile as she ushered everyone out the door.

Adelaide gave one last wave before the door closed in their faces.

"What's that about?" Tetsu asked.

"Maybe she wanted to be alone?" Kurt suggested.

"I don't think that's exactly it, Kurt," Adelaide said as she thought about Sophie's conversation with Darius earlier.

"Girls," Tetsu scoffed.

"Night, Kurt," Adelaide said as they paused outside his house. He waved goodbye and Tetsu and Adelaide continued up the street.

"You know I don't mean you, right?" Tetsu asked.

"What?" Adelaide asked confused.

"The thing about girls. I mean, you aren't like them. I like how you are."

"Thanks." A small smile crossed her otherwise impassive face. "They confuse me, too, you know."

They continued up the road in silence.

"All right, see ya!" Tetsu said as they reached her house. He waited at the side gate while she walked up the front steps and went into the house.

Adelaide took off her shoes and walked straight through the house to the kitchen. She waved at Tetsu as he opened the back gate and stepped out into the woods behind her house. Adelaide turned and appraised the kitchen with a sigh.

As usual, there were breadcrumbs on the counter and food debris on the floor.

She collected the broom from the cupboard, swept the detritus on the kitchen floor into a pile and then scooped it up into the dust pan. She dumped it into the garbage can and shook her head. The can was almost full again. She clipped the dustpan back on the broom and tucked them away in the cupboard. Adelaide wrestled the bag out of the garbage can, tied the top of it closed and set it by the back door. She grimaced at the memory of the last time she'd taken out the garbage.

"Howdy darlin'," Waylon said as he stepped into the kitchen. He took a glass from the cupboard and filled it with water. Adelaide watched as he drained the glass. Waylon placed the empty glass in the sink. "Oh, let me give ya a hand with that." He strode across the room and picked up the black garbage bag. "I'll take it with me on my way out."

"It's early for you to go to work," Adelaide observed. She didn't mind when Waylon was around.

"Sure is, but I told a friend I'd meet 'em for a coffee." Waylon smiled. It was warm and crooked. He always smelled of leather, although in the mornings the smell was mixed with stale beer. "You eaten yet?"

"Not yet. I think Mama is out with Rico. I'll heat up a can of soup in a bit."

"All right," Waylon said with a hint of hesitation. "Violet's upstairs, yeah? I know you know what you're doing, but you shouldn't be cooking unsupervised."

Adelaide nodded. "She is. I'll tell her before I turn on the stove."

"Okay then. And don't touch that glass. I'll wash it myself when I get home." Waylon indicated toward the sink.

"Okay. Thanks for that." Adelaide nodded at the garbage bag.

"My pleasure." Waylon tipped his cowboy hat with his free hand.

Adelaide listened to his footfalls as she pulled the mop and bucket out of the cupboard.

***

Darius appraised the pool house and nodded. He could line the counter with bowls of chips and stock the fridge with soda. If they moved the furniture around there would be an area to dance. He hoped people wanted to dance, but he suspected it would depend on the music. Adelaide had said she'd put together a mixed tape. Darius assured himself that if it wasn't any good, he could switch her tape out for one of his own. He hoped hers was good, but he knew a love of music didn't translate into a good mixed tape.

They'd invited both grade seven classes, which meant Davia would be there as well. There hadn't been a way to avoid it. Darius hoped his sister wouldn't ruin his plans. He wondered if Adelaide would kiss him again.

"Everything all right?" Miranda asked as she

stepped into the pool house.

"Yeah, Mom." Darius smiled. "Just working things out for the party."

"All right. You should order pizza for it. Make sure everyone has something to eat." She paused. "I'm glad you're making friends, Darius. We should get into the house, though. It's almost dinner time." She nodded toward the clock, which indicated it was almost six o'clock.

"Oh, sorry. I lost track of time."

"It's all right, Darius. Like I said, I'm glad you're making friends, but we shouldn't keep your father waiting."

Together, the two of them walked from the pool house back into the main building and took their seats at the long, antique wooden table. The table was laid with its usual collection of silverware and china plates, and a few platters of food had already been set out.

Davia walked in with their father a moment later just as Consuela carried a platter of stuffed game hens into the room and set it on the table.

The smell of sage and cilantro filled the room.

"Is there anything else I can get you, Mr. Belcouer?" Consuela asked.

"No, thank you," Drew said as he looked up at her.

Consuela smiled and inclined her head before she turned to Miranda. "Mrs. Belcouer. Anything else I can get you?"

"This looks wonderful, thank you," Miranda replied with a smile.

"What is that?" Davia pointed at a tray of brussels sprouts.

"They are roasted brussels sprouts glazed with spiced honey sauce, Miss Davia." Consuela smiled at her.

"Eww."

Consuela looked around the table, but her eyes settled on Darius who smiled. Consuela had yet to make a dish he didn't like. She smiled back at him.

"Davia," hissed Miranda. She turned to Consuela. "Thank you, Consuela. As always, it's wonderful."

Consuela inclined her head a final time and returned to the kitchen to start on the dishes.

"Manners," Drew growled at his daughter. "It's bad enough I have to put up with the idiot partners at the new office."

"Sorry, Daddy." Davia pouted.

"Treat your staff well. Always." Drew served himself mushroom and wild rice stuffing. "You know one of my employees didn't come in because he was attacked by a dog?" Drew shook his head. "Idiots. Next thing you know they'll be telling me birds attacked them."

Darius turned to his look at his father. He opened his mouth to speak when Davia cut in.

"But you pay the staff. Why do you have to be nice to them?"

Miranda closed her eyes. Darius fought back the urge to laugh.

"My staff? Because they are people, Davia." Drew looked at her.

"But you aren't nice to everyone," she pointed out.

Drew raised his eyebrows.

"I just mean,"—Davia searched for the words—"it isn't like you're nice to *everyone* all the time."

"Be good to the people you count on, Davia." Drew stabbed his hen and looked up at his daughter.

Darius cursed his sister for her interruption. He was desperate for more information about the dog attack, but he knew there was no point in asking his father now. Silver cutlery tapped against the china plates as the rest of the meal continued in silence.

Eight

Blondie chirped through the speakers in the pool house living room.

"Here, we could string this along that wall," Darius said as handed Adelaide the end of a roll of blue crepe paper. He wasn't sure the decorations were necessary, but it meant he had a reason to invite her over early.

"Okay," Adelaide said as she took the end of the roll.

Adelaide and Darius worked in silence as they affixed the crepe paper to the wall. "Heart of Glass" gave way to "We Got the Beat," and Adelaide swayed to the music while she worked. Darius watched for a moment, transfixed.

"Are you okay?" Adelaide asked.

She'd caught him staring.

"I got money from my dad for pizza," Darius said. He glanced over at the island in the kitchen. It was already covered with bags of chips and Consuela had put together several snack platters. "Do you think it'll be enough?"

"It's good." Adelaide said. Her voice was still monotone, but Darius thought he heard a hint of a smile.

"This mixed tape is pretty rad," Darius offered. He had been wrong to doubt her taste in music. Everything that played so far was something he had on his own mixed tapes, or wished he did.

"I know." Adelaide nodded. "I could make you a copy."

"I'd love that!" Darius grinned. "Or, uh, that'd be cool."

"What would be cool?" Davia asked as she flopped onto the couch.

"Hey Davia, we're just setting up," Darius said.

"Obviously." Davia rolled her eyes. "I hope this party isn't lame, Darius. I've got a lot riding on this."

"Right, well, it doesn't start for a bit, so maybe you could give us a hand?" Darius suggested. The first side of the tape finished, and Darius was surprised so much time had passed already.

"No, I'm good." Davia smiled.

Darius eyed his sister warily, then turned to Adelaide. "I'm just going to switch to side B."

The tape player was with the other stereo equipment in the pool house hallway closet. Darius flipped the cassette over, and scanned the liner. Adelaide had carefully written all of the songs in two columns. The songs were written in block text and the band names were missing. Her writing was tidy enough, Darius could easily read it, but it wasn't as delicate as most of the girls he had gone to school with. He set the cassette case back down on the tape player and pulled the closet doors closed.

Darius paused, glanced toward the main room, then grimaced. He was worried about leaving Davia alone with Adelaide for too long, but he was also fairly certain Adelaide could take care of herself. He stopped by the bathroom and returned to the living room a few moments later.

The Smith's "How Soon is Now" crooned through the speakers. Davia was still sprawled on the couch. Adelaide gave him a small smile. They both seemed much as they had before he left.

"Have you guys heard of the drug the high school students are using?" Davia asked. "Apparently it makes them sex maniacs. Like they just can't get enough." Davia turned to Adelaide. "Have you had sex?" Her tone was light, almost playful. "Darius will probably be a virgin forever."

Darius' eyes widened. He willed his sister to leave.

"No, I'm twelve." Adelaide frowned. "Have you?"

"Not yet, but I'm going to this year. Who wants to go to high school a virgin? Lame!" Davia shook her head.

"Why don't we pick out the pizza?" Darius interjected, desperate to change the subject.

"Sure, fine. Is there somewhere good to get pizza?" Davia raised her eyebrows.

"Yes," Adelaide said. "But it's kind of expensive."

Darius forced himself to take a breath. If he played it cool, maybe Adelaide would forget this whole conversation. He tried not to blush as he thought of Adelaide kissing him. "If it's the better place," Darius said with a shrug. "Do they deliver?"

"Just get something with meat on it for me," Davia said as she peeled herself off the couch. "I'm going to go get ready."

"Do you have a phonebook out here?" Adelaide asked.

Darius pulled one out of a drawer in the kitchen and Adelaide flipped the pages until she found the menu.

"Oceanside Pizzeria? This looks great!" Darius grinned as he scanned the menu. He'd never heard of prawns on pizza. Or pineapple with chicken.

"Darius?" Adelaide asked as she glanced at the door.

"Yeah?" Darius looked up and grinned.

"You said you got money from your dad for pizza, right?" Adelaide frowned.

"Yeah, yeah, don't worry about it. He was fine with it. We can get, probably ten of these. That should be enough, right?"

"That'll be enough." Adelaide's eyes widened. "That's very generous of him, but it's not that." She averted his gaze for a moment, then inhaled and looked at him. "Your mom came in while you were changing the tape. She gave Davia money for pizza."

"Really?" Darius was amused. He suspected his sister had done things like this in the past, but this was the first time he could confirm it.

"Yes. She gave her a wad of cash. I just don't want you to get in trouble."

"Pick out the best ones, okay? We'll get ten total. I'll be right back."

***

Darius returned a few minutes later and offered Adelaide some money.

"I can't take this," Adelaide shook her head at the

two twenty-dollar bills Darius held out to her.

"Sure, you can. I told Davia she had to split it with me. I wouldn't have known about it if you hadn't said something, so you get half of my half."

Adelaide hesitated. Darius' pool house was the same size as some of the houses on her street, and she'd never seen her fridge as full as the spare fridge in the pool house was. She looked down at the new sundress her mom had offered to buy her for the party. Under it was a new bathing suit. She'd wanted to decline both of them, to tell her mother to spend the money on groceries instead, but that wasn't how that worked. If she'd declined, the money would have been spent somewhere else and the cupboards would still be empty. Forty dollars could buy a lot of peanut butter and bread. She stuffed the bills into her pocket.

"Thank you. Your mom said she was going out." Adelaide thought back to the earlier visit.

"Yeah, she's going to the country club in Olympia. She doesn't want to be around a bunch of kids."

"What about the party?" Adelaide frowned. "Is your dad here?" Drew Belcouer intimidated her.

"He's in his office," Darius said. "At least that's the story."

"Aren't there going to be parents? We said there'd be parents." Adelaide's frown deepened.

"It's okay," Darius said. "Consuela, our cook, is in the house. And I won't let anything get out of hand."

Adelaide wasn't sure how he could be so confident. The idea of all of the people soon to arrive made her nervous, so she decided to change the subject. "That dog attack you told me about, do you think it could be at all related to the birds?"

Darius paused. "I dunno. I guess there's only one way to find out, though. This means we'll have to look into it."

Adelaide nodded. She felt warm as a grin spread across Darius' face. She marvelled at how easy it was to make him happy.

Nine

The music pumped through the speakers both in and outside of the pool house. Classmates lounged on patio furniture and wandered in and out of the pool house. A few kids sat on the edge of the pool and dangled their legs into the cool clear water.

"Hi Darius," Farrah batted her eyes.

"Hi Farrah." Darius smiled. "Hi Mrs. Turner."

"Hello, Darius. Can I speak with your parents?" Mrs. Turner looked around at the growing number of children.

"Mom," Farrah hissed.

"My mother is at the Club. You can speak to my father if you'd like Mrs. Turner. He is in the house, but he's on a call. He'll be out here shortly, but he asked that he not be interrupted. You're welcome to wait." Darius maintained eye contact and kept his voice steady.

"Well," Mrs. Turner glanced at her watch then at the house. She shook her head. "He *is* here?"

"He'd never leave us unsupervised." Darius crossed

81

his fingers behind his back.

"All right then. Call me if you need to be picked up early, honey," Mrs. Turner said to Farrah as she moved to the side gate.

"Your place is amazing," Farrah fawned. She was flanked by Julie and Ashley, who had their hair styled almost as big as Farrah.

"I guess so, thanks," Darius replied. He had lost track of Adelaide. He scanned the pool deck. Kurt scowled at him. Tetsu pulled his jeans off to reveal swim trunks.

"Like, the pool house has two floors," Julie said in awe.

"It came that way." Darius shrugged. He loved the pool house, but he was starting to feel uncomfortable about how much he had in comparison to most of his classmates. Back in Boston, everyone seemed to have more money than sense.

Julie giggled, seemingly oblivious.

"There's a bunch of soda in the fridge if you want some," Darius offered.

"Do you want to show me where it is?" Farrah fluffed her hair. Darius turned back to face her.

"It's right,"—Darius pointed inside the pool

house—"there. Help yourself."

Farrah gave a tight smile and turned toward the pool house.

"Hey!" Davia yelled from her chaise as she was splashed with water. A boy, Darius couldn't see who, had cannon-balled into the pool.

"First one in!" the boy yelled as he surfaced.

Davia turned back to the girls who had collected around her.

"This is a great party." Sophie put her hand on Darius' arm. He wasn't sure where she'd come from.

"Well, Adelaide helped me pull it off." Darius gave her a small smile.

"But this place," Sophie gestured. "So, rad."

"Thanks," Darius nodded. "Hey, have you seen Adelaide?"

"No." Sophie's face fell for just a moment. "Oh, I have to talk to them." Sophie gestured toward a group of people. Darius breathed a sigh of relief as she turned on her heel and walked away.

***

Adelaide grimaced as she jiggled the joystick on the

arcade machine. She pulled it back hard, but was too late. A few people behind her winced.

"That's rad!" Brody exclaimed.

"She died," Nelson pointed out.

Brody waved him away. "She got further than you." He turned to Adelaide and smiled. "How are you so good at this?"

"I'm not sure." Adelaide shrugged as she stepped back from the Frogger cabinet. "It was a good match, though."

"Not so fast." Brody pointed. "You set a new high score."

The fourth-place spot flashed on the screen. Adelaide could see the initials DAB in second, third and fifth place. In first place were the letters ADB. Adelaide maneuvered the joystick and entered A-W.

"Impressive," Darius said behind her.

"Thanks," Adelaide said. "Who is ADB?"

"That's my dad. Arthur Drewson Belcouer. He just goes by Drew. I imagine he won't play the game again unless we knock him off the top spot."

Adelaide wondered if Darius' father would come out to knock her score from the cabinet. She looked around. The party had grown in size. She could hear her classmates out on the pool deck. There were only a handful of people inside and most of them were eating pizza or watching people play Frogger.

"Rematch later?" Brody asked.

Adelaide nodded. She might not have romantic feelings for Brody, but she preferred Frogger with him to giggling by the pool deck.

"Spin the Bottle by the pool in ten!" Julie called as she walked through the main room of the pool house. "Spin the Bottle! Come on, Darius." Julie tugged at Darius' arm.

"Oh, I …" Darius looked over at Adelaide. "Are you playing?"

Adelaide imagined the bottle would land on Brody or Nelson if she spun it. She looked over and saw Brody's gaze on her.

Nelson had moved toward the pool deck, but even from behind, Adelaide knew it was him. He lifted his hand to push his thick glasses back up onto his nose, which was always scrunched in the vain hope the glasses wouldn't slide down. He had an unruly mop of blond hair and a nasal voice.

Nelson was taller than most of the boys in their grade, but he was thin and awkward. He didn't smell of body odour, but Adelaide still had no interest in his lips.

There was no way the bottle would land on Darius. No Seven Minutes in Heaven at a party would ever compare to the thrill of their first kiss. She'd stolen it in the closest of an office building while secret government agents prowled just outside.

"No," Adelaide said. She looked over at the counter and saw there were still a few boxes of pizza. "That's not my thing."

"Come on, Darius," Julie beckoned.

Adelaide walked to the counter and checked the pizza boxes. There were still slices of the tropical heat pizza. She loved the hot pepper and prawn combination. Pizza was a rare treat, but her mother shared her love of spicy food, and one thing Adelaide could say about her mother was she went all out. They never ordered from the cheaper chain pizza restaurant, just like they never shopped at Goodwill or bought generic brand food. Belinda Winter wanted the real thing, even if that cost more than she could afford.

Julie guided Darius across the room toward the pool deck. Adelaide closed her eyes and bobbed along to "Bad Reputation."

"Hey, Darius! This music is mint," Reggie called

from one of the couches.

"Adelaide put it together," Darius replied with a smile. "I can't take any credit for it."

"Great tunes," Colin said as he nodded at Adelaide.

"Thank you. Did you want some more pizza?" Adelaide asked.

"I'm good." Colin shook his head and turned back to Reggie. "But maybe that bag of chips."

The two of them looked relaxed on the sofa. Colin had his feet up on the coffee table. Reggie lounged with his back in the corner of the couch and his feet hung just off the seats.

Adelaide had heard them erupt into fits of laughter several times. She brought the bowl of ripple chips over and was struck by a piney and slightly skunky smell. She recognized it immediately.

"Got the munchies?" she asked as she handed the bowl over.

The two boys chuckled.

"Did you see Mrs. Anders' face?" Colin asked.

"Every day!" Reggie snorted.

Colin swatted him. "No, after the *thing*."

"What thing?" Adelaide asked.

Colin and Reggie snickered.

"The thing with her car," Colin explained when he caught his breath. He took a handful of chips and shoved them into his mouth.

"Did you two do it?" Adelaide asked in her monotone voice.

The boys erupted in a fit of laughter.

"Adelaide, hey," Kurt came up next to her.

"Hi Kurt." She turned. "Are you okay?"

"I just,"—he looked at Colin and Reggie and navigated Adelaide away from the couch—"don't know how to talk to Farrah." His cheeks reddened.

"Oh, just talk to her. Walk up and say 'Hello, Farrah. What do you think of the party?'"

"I can't," Kurt gaped.

"Sure, you can. You, Kurt Zillman, are a smart and caring person. You are one of my favourite people, and I know you can do this. You talk to me all the time. Just go talk to her." Adelaide indicated over toward Farrah. "It's a party, Kurt. Lots of people are chatting."

"Okay," Kurt said as he inhaled a big breath of air. "If you're sure."

"I am." Adelaide nodded. She watched as Kurt navigated around a group of people and walked toward Farrah.

He was in arm's reach of her when he tripped.

Kurt collided with Farrah, and the two of them tumbled into the pool.

Ten

There was an eruption of laughter. Kurt and Farrah flailed in the pool. Darius thought Kurt was trying to help her, but he wasn't a strong enough swimmer. He was about to jump in to help when the pair made it to the side of the pool.

Darius ducked away from Julie's grip. "You guys go ahead. I should help Kurt."

Before Darius could round the pool, Adelaide had a towel around Farrah. Her hair was flat, her dress was soaked, and makeup ran down her face.

"How could you do this Kurtis Zillman?" Farrah fumed. "Look what you've done!"

Adelaide made a pained face at Kurt, and then caught Darius' eye. She looked toward Kurt and Darius nodded. Darius saw Adelaide say something to Farrah and then the two of them walked toward the main house. A low chorus of laughter continued to roll across the pool deck.

"Hey, come on," Darius said as he reached Kurt.

"I'll help you get cleaned up."

"I don't deserve any help," Kurt mumbled. He looked like he wanted to curl up into a ball and die.

Darius put a hand on Kurt's shoulder and navigated him around the groups of kids toward the pool house. A boy with thick glasses and a nasal voice, Darius thought his name was Nelson, opened his mouth to say something. Darius looked at him. Nelson closed his mouth.

"I've got spare clothes in here." Darius led Kurt into the pool house.

"I can't believe I did that," Kurt mumbled. "She'll never talk to me now."

***

Adelaide led Farrah through a set of French doors into the Belcouer house. The room seemed to be some sort of sitting room with plush furniture.

"This way," Adelaide guessed as she exited the room into a hallway.

"Why are you in here?" a male voice demanded.

Adelaide jumped. She turned and saw Drew Belcouer. He was dressed in slacks and a neatly pressed dress shirt. In one hand he held a tumbler containing a finger's height of a dark amber beverage. She was sure Darius had said he wouldn't be here.

"Hello, Mr. Belcouer. I apologize for being in the main house. Farrah fell into the pool and needs a change of clothes." Adelaide kept her tone even, and she forced herself to maintain eye contact. "I was hoping to borrow something out of Davia's closet so Farrah could enjoy the rest of the party."

Drew appraised each of the girls with a scowl, then nodded. "Davia's room is up the stairs, the third door on the left." He turned and walked down the hall.

Adelaide breathed a sigh of relief and followed his directions. Everything about the house seemed ornate. Large paintings with thick frames hung in the hallway. The carpet underfoot was thick and plush. Even the ceilings seemed taller. They reached the entryway where a large painting of the Belcouer family looked out at them.

"That's creepy," Farrah whispered. "I mean, that's a big painting, right?"

Adelaide nodded, but said nothing, fearful Drew was lurking around another corner.

The pair climbed the wide set of stairs to the upper floor. The hallway here was just as fancy. A small table showcased a clear vase with a large colourful bouquet of flowers. A glance in the bathroom revealed coordinated plush towels and bars of ornately carved soap.

Davia's room was massive, with a four-poster bed, a pile of colourful stuffed animals, and Teen Beat magazine pinups. Emilio Estevez stared back at Adelaide next to a cabinet of mint condition My Little Ponies and half a dozen Barbies all propped up on plastic stands. There was a small bookshelf with a collection of pristine novels from various lines: *Sweet Dreams*, *Wildfire*, and *Sweet Valley High*. A brunette in a blue sweatband smiled up from the cover of *Nice Girls Don't*, which sat atop Davia's nightstand next to a clock radio and a dish of potpourri.

"What are you doing?" gaped Farrah as Adelaide opened the closet.

"You already know, Farrah." Adelaide sighed.

She didn't mind Farrah, and Kurt seemed to like her for whatever reason, but she couldn't stand stupid questions.

"I'm getting you clothing from Davia's closet." Adelaide gaped at the walk-in closet full of assorted clothing. "I don't think she'll even notice."

***

Darius surveyed the party from the bottom of the steps. He'd shown Kurt where some spare clothes were and given him an extra towel to dry off with.

Tetsu looked around and took a bottle of soda out of the fridge. Darius was sure it must have been his fourth one. He shook his head and wondered what sort of sugar high Tetsu would have.

Nelson pushed his way through the crowd and approached Darius. "Did Kurtis call his mother so he could be picked up early?" he asked in a nasal voice.

"I don't think we've met," Darius said. "I'm Darius."

"I know who you are," Nelson replied. He used his index finger to push his glasses up his nose. "This is your house. I'm Nelson. Nelson Unruh. You didn't answer my question. Did Kurtis call his mother?"

"No, he didn't." Darius appraised Nelson. He was dressed in canvas sneakers, jeans and a starched, checked button-down shirt. His tall skinny frame and mop of unruly blonde hair reminded Darius of the sparklers his father bought on Independence Day.

"Oh," Nelson said surprised. "That's good, I suppose. Thank you for the invitation. I find tonight quite enjoyable." He pushed the glasses up his nose. His gaze shifted to the stairs. "Kurtis. Welcome back."

Darius turned and smiled at Kurt. The black T-shirt was a bit large on him, but overall the clothes seemed to fit. Kurt had towel dried his hair and it was still damp and stuck up in several directions. Kurt sighed.

"Maybe I should call my mom. Can I use your phone, Darius?" Kurt asked.

"If that's what you want, but I think you should stick it out. It can't get worse."

"It could," Nelson countered. "It is foolish to assume just because something is bad it can't get worse."

"Right," Darius said with a slight frown. He turned back to Kurt. "You can do this. Chances are it won't get worse." He held up his hand as Nelson opened his mouth.

***

"Is that my dress?" Davia surveyed Farrah as she and Adelaide rejoined the party.

"Yes," Adelaide interjected. If Davia wanted to win the popular girls over at school, she'd need to either unseat or befriend Farrah. Adelaide wasn't certain which tactic Davia would choose, or which one would be better for Kurt, but she didn't like bullies. "We were sure you wouldn't mind."

Davia flicked her eyes from Farrah to Adelaide. She cocked her head a little to the left and surveyed Adelaide.

Adelaide met her eyes and didn't look away. She thought back to when she had met Miranda earlier in the day and when she had run into Drew inside the house. She had felt each of the Belcouers appraise her as though they could determine her worth from a single look. Each of them except Darius.

Davia averted her gaze first. "That's fine," she said as she looked back at Farrah. She plastered a smile across her face. "It looks good on you and I never really wear it. You can just keep it."

"Thanks, Davia," Farrah gushed. "I really appreciate it. And thanks for your help, Adelaide."

"You're welcome." Adelaide gave Farrah a small smile. She could smell cigarette smoke wafting off of Davia. She couldn't imagine Drew was the kind of man who wanted his daughter to smoke. Adelaide turned to face Davia and met her gaze again. "You didn't tell me your dad was back."

Adelaide felt a strange sense of satisfaction as the colour drained from Davia's face.

***

The bottle landed on Sophie, and Tetsu grimaced.

Sophie didn't look any happier. "Let's get this over with," she muttered.

The two of them crawled to the centre of the circle and shared a brief, chaste kiss. Darius knew Davia would play Spin the Bottle, and the last thing he needed was the bottle to point to her. There was only one girl he wanted to kiss, and she wasn't playing.

"Come on, Adelaide," Brody called. "You could still join us. There's space for both of you."

Darius looked hopefully at Adelaide who waved her hand.

"No thanks, I'm good here."

Sophie spun the bottle, and it landed on a boy named Ritchie. Their kiss was just as chaste and Davia heaved a sigh.

"That's not how to do it," she moaned. She leaned forward and took the bottle before Ritchie could. "Let me show you."

Davia spun the bottle. It went around and around, and then landed on Kurt. Davia grinned and crawled forward. She beckoned with one of her fingers. "Pucker up," she cooed.

Davia crawled across the whole circle, sat up, and

pulled Kurt in. She put one hand behind his head and opened his mouth with hers.

When she pulled away, Kurt's cheeks were flaming red.

Davia licked her lips and crawled back to her spot.

"What is she up to?" Adelaide murmured.

"My sister?" Darius asked. "Who knows? Are you having fun?"

"I am," Adelaide said. "Thanks for helping Kurt."

"Oh, sure," Darius said. He hadn't thought twice about it, even if Kurt had scowled at him earlier.

"Kurt likes Farrah," Adelaide said. "Farrah seems to like you. A lot of the girls do."

Darius turned to study her. Her face was impassive, but it was as if she'd sensed his question about Kurt. He wondered how she could answer those unasked questions, but not make it clear if she was one of the girls who liked him. She'd kissed him, but she'd also made it clear she didn't want a boyfriend.

"The music is great. I think the party is a success."

"It really is." Adelaide offered a smile. "Our party is a success."

Darius liked the way she used the word our, as though they shared something.

***

A street light illuminated the inside of the white K-car as Belinda drove beneath it. She'd purchased the vehicle off a used lot about a year prior, but in that time, she'd made it her own. There were plenty of new dents and scratches on the exterior; evidence of rogue swipes of a mascara wand while driving streaked the car ceiling; a collection of half-used lipsticks filled the central console; and a bottle of hand lotion had seeped through a partially closed cap and permanently scented the car with artificial roses. Still, Adelaide knew how proud her mother was of the car.

A light rain pattered on the windshield. The raindrops on Adelaide's window danced their way toward the ground. Adelaide watched as they descended down the pane. She smiled as the drops collected the smaller drops beneath them until they were strong enough to make little rivers that flowed off the window. Belinda bobbed her head along to "A Forest" by The Cure. When the song came to an end, she turned down the volume.

"Was it a good party, baby?" Belinda asked. The front wipers swooshed across the windshield.

"Yes, it really was." Adelaide smiled out the car

window at the dark houses. She considered herself lucky the rain held out as long as it did.

"How were his parents?" Belinda asked.

"His mother is strange. She asked how tall you were." Adelaide frowned.

"Really?" Belinda chuckled.

"Really. She looked like she wanted to eat me up," Adelaide recalled in an even tone.

"Rich people. What did Darius say?" Belinda asked as she fiddled with the switch for the heater.

"Oh, he wasn't there at the time. He'd gone to change the cassette." Adelaide turned her attention back to the raindrops on her window.

"Hmm, well, did you kiss any boys? Darius maybe?" Belinda teased.

"No, no kissing, Mama." Adelaide looked back over at her mother and thought she looked disappointed. "Sophie and Tetsu kissed. It was a pretty small one. And Davia made out with Kurt."

"Little Kurt Zillman?" Belinda gasped dramatically.

"Kurt from up the road, yes." Adelaide smiled slightly at her mother's enthusiasm. "He looked quite surprised. It was Spin the Bottle. She's up to something and I don't like it."

Belinda chuckled.

"What?" Adelaide demanded. She hated when her mother laughed at her.

"Well, of course she is, baby. Davia is a popular girl, right?" Belinda turned on her indicator.

"She wants to be. I suspect she was at her old school."

"Of course, she was. But I bet she's not smart. At least not book smart." Belinda turned the corner. "But she is smart enough to know that Kurt is smart and that having him as a friend, or at least getting him to like her, will pay off in the long run. It's ..." Belinda trailed off searching for the right words. "It's a calculated investment, that's it."

"A 'calculated investment?'" Adelaide frowned.

"Yep, that's the best way to say it. Fancy, right?" Belinda asked, proudly.

A dog's baying caused Adelaide to stiffen. It sounded angry, and close. She glanced over at her mother who frowned, then shook her head, as if dismissing the noise. Adelaide remained unsettled, but she tried to push the sounds from her mind.

"You're probably right," Adelaide admitted with a frown. She didn't want Kurt to be used.

"Trust me on this," her mother said as she patted Adelaide's leg. "It's what I would have done."

Eleven

"I'm just saying, what if he becomes popular now?" Tetsu garbled as he shoveled another spoonful of Froot Loops into his mouth.

"Because Davia kissed him?" Adelaide frowned.

"Yeah, because Davia kissed him." A trickle of milk ran out of Tetsu's mouth.

"Kissing a girl as foxy as Davia is gonna make people notice Kurt. Mark my words!"

"We'll see," Adelaide said as she rinsed her bowl out. "Tell me again why you wore your jeans over your swim trunks to the party?"

"So my mom wouldn't see! You think she'd let me go to a pool party? It's probably forbidden." Tetsu lifted the bowl to his mouth and tipped it back.

"She isn't that bad, Tetsu."

"She doesn't make you eat rice for breakfast," Tetsu said as he slurped his milk.

"Oh, I forgot. I might have a lead on who is responsible for the damage to Mrs. Anders' car."

"Really?" Tetsu looked up from his bowl, intrigued.

"Colin and Reggie know something," Adelaide replied.

"No way those two stoners actually accomplished anything." Tetsu scoffed.

"They know something," Adelaide insisted. "I just got pulled away from them at the party and didn't find out what."

"I'll take care of it," Tetsu assured her with an eerie sense of authority.

"What does that mean?" Adelaide asked in her even tone. The two of them stared at each other until Tetsu looked away first.

"It means I'll go ask them," Tetsu relented. "I was just trying to sound cool. Why can't you let me have that?"

"I'm sorry, Tetsu," Adelaide said with a grimace. She sighed as a feeling of guilt settled over her.

***

"How was your party, dear?" Miranda asked. She sat at the table in her purple spandex leggings and teal spandex top with her robe pulled over. A plate of breakfast was arranged in front of her.

"It was good. Really good." Darius grinned.

"That's wonderful." Miranda spooned a segment of grapefruit. "Adelaide seems delightful."

Darius almost laughed. "She's pretty great," he replied. Wonderful as she was, Darius wasn't sure he'd ever use the word delightful to describe her.

"You should invite her over for dinner soon. Then we can all get to know her a bit better."

"Soon, maybe." Darius crossed his fingers behind his back. He tried to imagine making Adelaide suffer through a Belcouer family dinner. "I think I'll make eggs. Do you want eggs?" Darius offered.

"Do you know how to cook them?" Miranda asked with a frown.

"I'm about to find out!" Darius grinned.

***

Adelaide stood outside Rutledge's with a newspaper in hand. She frowned at the headline "Dog Stops Home Invasion."

"You gotta stop with that. Comics, Adelaide. Comics. They are way more interesting." Tetsu twisted the top off a bottle of soda and took a swig.

"There's an article on a dog attack in here. I heard one howling after the party last night. And there were those other reports."

"So? Who cares about a dog attack?" Tetsu asked as he juggled his soda and popped several candies into his mouth. His tone was light, but there was an unfamiliar edge to it.

"Yes, right here." Adelaide glanced up and appraised Tetsu who was chewing the candies loudly. She looked back down and scanned the article. "A man was attacked by a dog while allegedly breaking into a house. The dog came at him from behind." Adelaide frowned.

There was a long pause. "Ha! From behind." Tetsu snorted.

"Grow up," Adelaide replied, though she still had the nagging feeling something was off about Tetsu. He didn't usually wait until he'd swallowed the food in his mouth to crack a joke. "The housekeeper came out to see what the ruckus was. It sounds like he'd done work on the house the previous week. The dog was described as 'a big black dog with a metal collar.' It didn't live at the residence, and it took off before anyone could get it."

"How many of these do you think I can fit in my

mouth at once?" Tetsu asked as he studied the bag of candy.

"Too many, and not enough all at once," Adelaide said as she tucked the paper into her backpack. Raindrops started to fall. "Let's get back."

***

"So, is Adelaide your *girlfriend* yet?" Davia prodded.

"Is Kurt your boyfriend?" Darius fired back as he climbed out of the pool.

"Did you *kiss* her? Did you *call* her yet? 'Oh, Adelaide, I'm in *love* with you,'" Davia mocked.

"It's a wonder you have any friends." Darius rolled his eyes as he toweled himself off.

"I have lots of friends." Davia scowled.

"Sure, you do. I'm pretty sure half of them are scared of you, and the other half just want your money."

"So? I'm going to be popular this year, Darius. You and this stupid little town aren't going to ruin that for me, you got it?" Davia stood to her full height. Darius was sure it was meant to be imposing, but her short stature did little to intimidate him. Her eyes, however, fumed with rage.

"I'm going out, Davia. I don't really care what you do," Darius said. He knew better than to be around her when she got like this.

***

Adelaide sat down on one of The Diner's red patent-leather benches across from Darius. The low hum of dozens of conversations drowned out the jukebox on the other side of the restaurant.

"You made it!" Darius said with a grin.

"I said I would when you called." Adelaide pulled the newspaper clipping about the dog attack from her pocket. "You know how you like weird stuff? I don't know if this is anything, but it might be."

Darius took a look at the clipping and grinned. "I was looking at this, too. We should investigate it together."

Adelaide nodded. "I'd like that. Where do we start? I actually heard it near your place after the party."

"Really? I wonder how I missed it." Darius grimaced. "We could just bike around," he proposed. He doubted it would be effective, but it had worked in the past.

"Let's keep an eye out for another attack," Adelaide suggested as she picked up her milkshake. "Maybe we can find a pattern to its movements. In the meantime, though, we could just go for a bike ride."

Darius raised his glass. "Cheers to that!"

Twelve

Adelaide awoke with a start. Her bedroom was dark. The digital red numbers on her clock radio indicated it was after two in the morning. She looked around, not certain why she'd awoken.

A guttural howl, echoing from the woods, caused her to shudder. The hair on her arms stood on end.

Adelaide pulled her covers up closer to her chin and sought refuge in her warm bed. She forced herself to take a deep breath and reasoned that whatever had made the noise, couldn't possibly get to her inside the house.

Adelaide crept out of bed toward the window. She pulled open the curtains and peered out into the darkness. She could make out the shapes of the trees closer to their fence line and the shed in the back corner of the yard. She held her breath and scanned the area for any sign of moment.

The old wooden floorboards in the hallway creaked and Adelaide stiffened.

Her door opened.

"Are you okay, baby?" her mother asked.

Adelaide exhaled the breath she'd been holding. "I'm okay, Mama," Adelaide said, her tone even. "Did I wake you?"

"No. That noise did," Belinda said with a shudder. She moved into the room and closed the door behind her.

There was another long, deep howl. Adelaide thought it sounded closer. She glanced toward the window, but she still couldn't see what was making the noise.

"Did you want me to cuddle up with you?" Belinda asked.

"Sure, Mama," Adelaide said, amused. Her mother needed the company more than she did. Adelaide climbed back into bed and Belinda climbed in next to her and pulled her close.

"I'm here, baby. Back to sleep," Belinda said.

"Okay, Mama," Adelaide said, as she stroked her mother's arm.

Belinda stiffened as another howl broke the silence.

"Shh, shh," Adelaide cooed. "It can't get inside."

"Of course, it can't," Belinda agreed as she settled herself back into the mattress.

***

Monday morning hadn't come soon enough. Darius sat at the kitchen table, eager to get through the school day and begin his investigation of the dog attacks.

"Here you are, Mr. Darius," Consuela smiled as she set a plate in front of Darius. Faint tendrils of steam rose from the pile of scrambled eggs and sausages. Next to them was a little dish of colourful fruit salad. Darius salivated.

"Thank you, Consuela." Darius smiled at her as he unfolded a cloth napkin onto his lap.

"Of course, Mr. Darius. Would you like more coffee Mr. Belcouer?"

"Yes, thank you." Drew looked up from his paper. "Why isn't your sister eating yet, Darius? We have to leave soon."

"I don't know. Maybe she's still doing her makeup." Darius scooped eggs onto his fork. He wondered if those girls he'd overheard at school could give him any more information.

Drew sighed. "I'm not going to be late." He set the paper down and got up from the table.

Darius could hear his father's footfalls in the

hallway, and then up the stairs. He noticed one of the headlines open on the page "Birds Dive Bomb Picnic." Darius stood and walked around the table. The article was small. A family was attacked by a flock of birds at a park near Seattle. Most of the birds were seagulls, but the parents claimed an eagle attempted to carry their six-year-old daughter away in its talons. He wondered if the two cases could be related.

"Come on, Daddy," Davia huffed from the hallway.

"No child your age needs that much makeup."

***

Adelaide rubbed her eyes as she stepped outside and closed the front door of her house. Tetsu, who had knocked moments before, fell in step with her as she descended the porch steps.

"Did you hear them?" Tetsu asked.

"How could I not?" Adelaide appraised the rain and walked down her driveway to the street. "The howls were incessant." She recalled how the howling dog had caused her mother to spend most of the night in a restless slumber in Adelaide's room.

"Think they were close?" Tetsu asked.

There was an edge to his voice.

"Yes. The howls came from the woods. It might have been one, possibly two dogs. I couldn't tell." She started down the road to the bus stop and wondered if the dog would make its presence known on the way there. The howls had stopped some hours ago. She hadn't expected Tetsu to be so worried about whatever the creature was, but before she could ask him about it, Kurt scampered out of his house.

He scurried down the front walkway of the Zillman house and didn't look back. "Let's go." Kurt indicated to keep moving and led them just past Sophie's driveway. The trio stopped where a large rhododendron blocked their view of Kurt's front window.

"Do you think it's a wolf?" Tetsu asked.

"Is what a wolf?" Kurt asked. He glanced nervously back toward his house, then ducked behind the bush again.

"The dog howling in the woods last night," Adelaide explained.

"I doubt it. The wolf population is on the decline."

"Plus the newspaper reported a black dog. I think the wolves you might find in Washington state are grey. Is that right?" Adelaide checked with Kurt, who nodded.

"You okay, man?" Tetsu asked.

"I'm fine," Kurt insisted. "But we should get going if Sophie isn't here in a second. We could miss the bus."

Adelaide gave Kurt a small but reassuring smile and wondered how bad it had been in the Zillman house this morning.

"I'm here!" Sophie called as she bounded down her front steps toward them.

"Let's go," Kurt urged and the group carried on toward the bus stop.

***

"Why do we have to be here so early?" Davia moaned next to him.

"Why not?" Darius shrugged. He wanted to point out they were not in fact early, and that Davia had caused them to be dropped off later than usual, but thought better of it. There was every chance Davia just wished school started closer to noon.

"This is about your girlfriend isn't it?"

"Don't you have friends you should be brainwashing?" Darius retorted as he watched the school bus pull in.

"You think you're so funny." Davia rolled her eyes.

Adelaide was one of the first people off the bus and Darius fell into step with her right away. Davia moved up next to Kurt and took his arm. Darius almost stopped dead in his tracks. Kurt looked at Adelaide, and Darius thought he saw her nod just once before Kurt let Davia lead him away. Darius shook his head.

"Hi!" He grinned at Adelaide. "How was the rest of your weekend?"

"It was weird, actually." She smiled, but her voice was monotone.

"Oh yeah?" Darius asked.

"Yes." Adelaide nodded. "I heard the dog. It was near my house."

"No way! Did you see it? We have to check it out!" Darius exclaimed with a grin. "In the woods? Maybe I can come over after school? My dad could give you a ride."

"She's not going into the woods with you," Tetsu scoffed.

"Are you going to come keep us safe?" Darius asked.

"I have karate practice. You guys should just skip it." Tetsu tried to keep Darius' gaze but averted his eyes.

Adelaide pursed her lips into a small frown.

"Your house," Darius said to Adelaide with a nod.

"After school."

Adelaide nodded in agreement. "Looking forward to it."

"This is a bad idea," Tetsu warned. "Remember that I told you it was a bad idea," he said to Adelaide. He just shook his head at Darius.

Thirteen

The day seemed longer than most, and Darius fought the urge to grab Adelaide's hand as he hurried her out of the classroom to his father's Town Car.

"Hey, Dad!" Darius scurried to the open window and ran his hand through his mop of hair. "Can I please spend the afternoon at Adelaide's? I could ride the bus over there. You could pick me up later. Or her mom could drive me home."

"Slow down, Darius," Drew said as he opened the car door and stepped out. He frowned toward the school, then looked back at Adelaide. "Is your mother going to be okay with this?"

"Yes, Mr. Belcouer. She won't mind," Adelaide assured him. "I'm sure she'd be happy to give Darius a ride home."

Darius held his breath.

Drew narrowed his eyes and appraised her. "Fine, get in the car." He gestured at the door. "I'll drive you there. Darius, where is your sister?"

"I'm not sure, Dad." Darius grinned as he climbed into the backseat and turned to Adelaide. "This is going to be so rad!"

A few minutes later, Davia strolled to the car and climbed into the front seat. She craned her neck and looked back at the two of them. When Adelaide pulled her seatbelt on, Davia puckered her lips and made kissy faces at Darius. Even that couldn't spoil his mood.

Drew honked as he pulled out of the stall. Darius looked out the window and noticed a car was inches away from theirs. He grimaced at how close they had been to a collision.

"Idiot drivers," his dad muttered as he shifted out of reverse. "Where do you live?"

"997 Pine Street, Mr. Belcouer," Adelaide said. "Do you need directions?"

"No," Drew shook his head and put on his indicator. "You're near the woods then, aren't you?"

"Yes, Mr. Belcouer."

"What are the two of you doing this afternoon?" Drew looked at them through the rearview mirror.

"School project," Darius interjected. "We have to work on our presentation about marsupials."

Drew eyed him with suspicion, but let it go. His

gaze flicked to Adelaide. "What is your mother's name?"

"Belinda. Belinda Winter."

"And what does she do for work?" Drew glanced in the rearview mirror again.

"She's currently unemployed. But she'll have a new job soon," Adelaide added. "She should be at home if you'd like to meet her."

Drew nodded. "Your father's name?"

"Cole. Cole Coyne."

"And what does he do?" Drew made a right turn, his indicator clicking away.

"I can't really say. Everyone says he's dead. He was MIA after the war in Vietnam." Adelaide's voice remained even.

Darius wanted to tell his father to stop.

"I see, well, I'm sorry to hear that," Drew said as he looked at her in the rearview again.

Adelaide's house, a big old Colonial Revival at the end of the street, had called to Darius the moment he'd seen it. He sucked his breath in in anticipation. Today he'd finally be able to see inside the house.

Drew eased the car down the road and pulled into the driveway.

"Thanks, Dad!" Darius called as he climbed out.

He grimaced as his father opened the driver's side door. The three of them walked up the saggy front steps to the porch, where Adelaide pulled out a key.

"Mama," Adelaide called as she opened the door. "I'm home."

"Is that you, baby?" A brunette woman, Darius guessed she couldn't have been older than thirty, bounded down the long wooden staircase in underwear and an oversized T-shirt. Her eyes widened as she realized Adelaide wasn't alone.

"Darius came over," Adelaide said in her monotone voice.

"So I see. Hello, uh, Mr. Belcouer." Belinda held her hand out and smiled.

"Ms. Winter," Drew said. He took her hand and shook it.

"Okay, bye Dad," Darius called.

"Come on, this way," Adelaide said as she led Darius farther into the house.

An assortment of paintings and picture frames hung on the walls. The tall baseboards were made of a dark wood that hadn't been polished in a very long time. Darius could still hear his father talking to Adelaide's mother as they made their way into the kitchen. It was a large room with a banquette and a sturdy wooden table.

"As soon as he goes we can head out," Adelaide gestured to the backdoor.

The yard was smaller than the one at his new home, but Darius guessed it was expansive for the area. He could make out a tired wooden shed, an unkempt garden, and overgrown grass. Along the perimeter of the yard was a tall, sturdy but faded, wooden fence with a big gate.

"That is so rad," Darius said as he nodded. "I love your house." He looked around the kitchen at the dark green linoleum floor and the plain white cabinets. A green can of MJB sat next to the coffee machine and a flowery ceramic jar crammed with cooking implements rested next to the mustard-yellow stove. The fridge, a matching mustard yellow, was decorated with oversized magnets and a shopping list. Along one wall was a large built-in bench, a sturdy wooden table and two chairs.

The front door closed.

"I'm just going to get dressed, baby!" Belinda called from the front hallway.

"It's fine, Mama," Adelaide called back in her monotone. "We're going out for a walk in the woods. Don't worry, we'll stick together."

Darius was still marvelling at the kitchen when

Adelaide ushered him outside and closed the back wooden door behind them. They stepped out onto a small porch, and Darius followed Adelaide down the steps and across the yard.

She punched a few keys on a pad on the gate, and swung it open. "Come on."

Darius breathed in the piney scent that hung in the air. Somewhere in the distance, a pair of birds chirped at each other. While none of the branches reached over Adelaide's fence, some of them were quite close. As soon as Darius stepped through the gate it was as though he was transported deep into a mystical forest.

"I love it." Darius grinned. "Which way should we go? Which direction did the howls come from?" Darius saw a narrow trail that skirted her fence line and led off to the right, but there was also one that went deeper into the forest.

"That way?" Adelaide guessed and pointed into the woods. The two fell in stride.

The forest was quiet and peaceful and Darius wondered if it was possible for them to find anything at all. Part of him hoped they would, but spending time alone with Adelaide was more than a consolation and he wasn't exactly certain what to do if they did find the beast making headlines in the newspaper.

They walked for some time, under the canopy of trees. Darius fought the urge to take Adelaide's hand.

"I love it out here," Adelaide said.

Branches and bracken cracked under their feet but the forest seemed otherwise still.

"It's so quiet," Darius remarked.

"I suppose. Listen closer," Adelaide said. She stopped walking, looked up at the canopy and sighed. A small smile played at her lips.

Darius watched her as he listened. In the distance, small birds chirped. Somewhere farther away than that, Darius thought he heard running water. A bug zipped past his ear.

A crow cawed loudly nearby.

Adelaide frowned as her eyes snapped open.

A black shape dove toward them, its wings beating furiously.

"Get down!" Adelaide dropped to her knees, tucked her head, and threw her hands protectively over the back of her neck.

Darius cast his gaze around. The sounds of bugs and chirping was drowned out by the beating of wings and his own heart pounding in his ears. His eyes fell on a fallen tree branch.

The crow dove straight toward Adelaide who had tucked herself into a ball.

Darius scrambled for the branch. The ground was uneven and he stumbled.

The crow screamed.

The black shape was on top of Adelaide now.

Darius staggered forward and his fingers closed around the rough bark.

Adelaide called out as the bird clawed at her back with its talons.

A shiver rolled down Darius' spine. He righted himself, gripped the branch and swung. His foot slipped on the wet ground and his swing went wide, missing the bird and almost hitting Adelaide.

The bird, sensing the assault, let go of Adelaide and flew up several feet. It cawed loudly, then dove toward her again.

Darius steadied himself and adjusted the grip on the branch. He swung again. This time it connected with the bird.

It was flung backward, where it hit the ground. Within seconds, it had spread its wings and was back up in the air.

"Get out of here!" Darius called as he thrust the branch at the crow. "Get!" He pulled himself to his full height and stepped toward the bird, brandishing the makeshift club. Darius hesitated as the crow's malicious eyes appraised him.

The bird beat its wings and flew straight at Darius.

Darius braced himself, then swung the branch out at the creature.

The bird, as if anticipating his movements, rose up several feet out of reach.

The swing missed.

The crow cawed. The light glinted off its eyes as it redirected itself toward the ground, straight toward Darius.

Darius sucked in his breath. He knew he needed to move, but his feet wouldn't cooperate. His arms, too, were unwilling to move. He was frozen.

The crow closed the distance and dove straight for Darius' face.

It was within inches of him now. Still, he was unable to move.

The bird's feathers were glossy and black. Its eyes radiated an unnatural rage.

Darius willed himself to run but his legs felt like

spaghetti noodles. Something slammed into Darius' side and he toppled to the ground. The smell of rotting leaves and damp earth assaulted his nostrils. His side hurt, but it was a dull pain. He twisted his body and realized Adelaide had tackled him.

The bird aborted its attack, flew up another few feet and circled them.

Adelaide scrambled off Darius and snatched up a rock.

Darius clambered to his feet, picked up the branch and waved it around. "Get out of here!" he called.

The bird circled once more, then let out one last caw before it turned and flew off into the trees.

"Are you okay?" Darius turned to Adelaide.

"I'll be fine," Adelaide said. "I'm sorry for tackling you."

"I'm okay." He rubbed his side, surprised at how strong she was.

"Thank you for …" She gestured at the branch and winced.

"Oh, sure. Are you sure you're okay?"

"I don't think it's deep," she replied. "I'll be okay."

"Let me take a look," Darius said, worriedly.

Adelaide pursed her lips, then nodded. She turned

and lifted up her jacket and shirt.

The fabric hadn't been torn, and Darius hoped that was a good sign. He reached out and helped Adelaide pull the clothing away from her back so he could take a look. There were a few little pink lines, but it didn't look like the skin had been broken. "I think you're right. Maybe a bit of cream or something when we get back."

He gently pulled the shirt and jacket back down.

Adelaide nodded. "Okay."

"Um … that wasn't normal, right?" Darius asked.

Adelaide sighed. "I wouldn't say it's normal, but it has happened before. The other day actually."

"And you didn't say anything?" Darius asked, incredulous.

"I meant to." Adelaide frowned. "Then you were late to school and Tetsu needed my help."

"So? What happened?"

"I'd taken the garbage out and a crow dive bombed me. Like what just happened. Only when I ducked down it hit the side of the house. Hard. It didn't get back up." She led Darius along the deer trail they were following. "Of course, there's no house here for it to plow into so my plan wasn't that good."

"That's crazy! You're sure you're okay?" Darius

reached out and put his hand on Adelaide's arm.

She paused, then turned and smiled at him. "I'm okay."

"It must be related to the bird man," Darius declared.

"You're probably right," Adelaide said as she glanced up into the tree canopy. "I thought he'd left the area, but maybe there were still some birds here."

Darius nodded and grinned. "Maybe we can still get some answers! Here! Look at this!" They had followed the trail as it curved around the trunk of a large tree. "See it?" He strode over to a nearby tree and pointed out a paw print in the soft ground.

"I do." Adelaide moved closer. "So we just have to find—"

She was cut off midsentence as a branch snapped with a sharp report somewhere nearby.

Fourteen

"Hello?" Darius called. He stepped forward and put himself between Adelaide and the direction the noise had come from. "Hello? We know you're there."

"Hello!" a woman called as she emerged from the trees. She carried a black helmet in one hand and a rifle in the other. She was dressed in jeans and an oversized dark brown bomber jacket.

"What are you doing here?" Adelaide asked.

"I'm just out for a hike. What about you kids? It's dangerous out here, you know." The woman's tone was light.

"We're hiking. Where's your bike?" Adelaide pointed at her helmet.

"Back on the main road." She smiled. "I like the call of the wild."

The woman was of average height, and plain looking. Even with her oversized jacket on, she looked thin and unimposing.

"I'm not sure it's safe to hunt out here." Adelaide

eyed the rifle. "Kids could be hiking."

"This?" The woman nodded at the rifle. "Just a tranquilizer gun. I'm hunting bears."

"Bears? Not dogs?" Darius asked.

"Bears," the woman said as she glanced around. "You kids should run along."

Suddenly, out of nowhere, Darius lunged at the woman. His hands wrapped around the barrel of the gun and he pulled. The woman's grip was tight, and the two wrestled over the firearm, which pointed up toward the sky.

"Darius!" Adelaide called. She wasn't sure if she'd missed his signal or he'd just acted without thinking, but she knew this wasn't going to end well. "Stop!"

There was a low growl from the underbrush.

Adelaide sucked in her breath and froze.

"Don't! You have to let go!" the woman screamed; her casual façade gone. "You'll trigger it!"

"Darius," Adelaide warned as another growl emerged from behind a nearby rotting log. It was closer now.

Darius hesitated and the woman shoved him. He fell onto the ground, landing on his rear end.

Adelaide ran to his side as a large black dog with a

metal collar moved out from the underbrush. Its lips were pulled back revealing sharp teeth. Saliva slowly dripped from its jowls.

"Come on, come here, it's all right." The woman beckoned.

The dark beast growled again and raised its hackles.

"What is it?" Darius gaped from the ground.

The creature's leg and snout were covered with exposed grey metal, and something about its eyes was wrong.

Adelaide didn't take her eyes off the creature, but she sensed Darius start to get to his feet.

It looked like it had been a dog once. Adelaide could see now all four of its legs were partially made of metal. The dog's thick black coat still covered portions of its legs.

The dog's head swivelled and its eyes focused on Darius.

Adelaide sucked in her breath.

The dog turned and looked at Adelaide, but she felt it dismiss her and it turned its attention back to Darius and the woman. It looked between the two of them and let out another long low growl.

"I made it. It's what I was out here to find. You

should really go, just walk away slowly." The woman moved closer to the dog.

Its growl deepened.

"We're not leaving," Darius said with a slight quaver to his voice. "How'd you make it?"

The woman sighed and turned her gaze to Darius. She opened her mouth to say something, but before she could get a word out, the dark beast leapt into the air.

The woman didn't have a chance to scream as the creature pushed her to the ground, knocking the wind out of her.

Adelaide clapped a hand over her mouth, her eyes wide.

The woman had her arms up and the gun, gripped tightly in each hand, served as a shield to keep the dog at bay. Still, its snout was close to her face. Tendrils of saliva dripped from its mouth. It growled again, low and deep.

"Help! Please!" the woman gasped.

Adelaide cast her gaze around. Her heart pounded in her chest.

Darius was already on the move. He snatched up a rock and brought his arm back, as if to throw it.

"Stop!" Adelaide demanded. She hoped she was right. "Stop," she repeated as she looked at Darius.

Darius hesitated. He looked between Adelaide and the melee occurring on the ground. "We have to help her."

"You said he'd trigger it, what does that mean?" Adelaide couldn't keep the edge of panic from her voice. She was only mostly certain the dog didn't see her as a threat. Her heart raced in her chest, fearful of what she'd have to witness if she couldn't stop the creature.

The woman grunted and strained, holding the dog inches from her face. "Guilt. It's triggered by guilt," she groaned.

"That's why it growled when you were trying to take her gun," Adelaide guessed. She was thinking as fast as she could, desperate for a solution. "Apologize to it!"

"What?" the woman exclaimed.

The dog twisted. It brought its maw down toward the woman's shoulder.

"Watch out!" Darius yelled as the woman shoved the dog and rolled out of the way.

The beast's face almost hit the ground, but it caught itself and clambered to its feet.

The woman scrambled to her feet as well, but she wasn't quite as fast. Her hands, shaking with fright, fumbled with the gun. It dropped to the ground.

Fifteen

The woman bent to reach the gun.

The dog growled and stepped toward the woman, its teeth bared.

"Don't do that. You've upset it," Adelaide warned in a raised whisper. "You've upset it and you feel guilty. Apologize."

"To the dog?" the woman asked.

"It's as good a plan as any," Darius chimed in. He moved slowly toward Adelaide, his eyes still on the creature. His grip tightened on the rock in his hand. He didn't want to hurt it, but he couldn't let it hurt Adelaide.

The beast growled again. Its body was tense, ready to pounce.

"I ... I'm sorry," the woman stuttered. "I didn't want them to hurt you, and I put you out here and I ..." Her eyes flicked toward Darius and Adelaide, then back toward the creature. "I thought you'd be safe. I thought it would be better ..."

The dog's growl quieted, but its body was still tense,

its eyes still firmly affixed on the woman.

"Keep going," Adelaide urged.

Darius' heart raced. His palms were sweating.

"I'm sorry," the woman repeated. "I was trying to save you. I was really trying to save you. They'd have exterminated you."

The creature relaxed with that, but Darius could sense it was still wary. It sniffed at the air.

"Come on," Adelaide coaxed. "Come here. I'm not going to hurt you." She crouched down as she moved forward.

The beast cocked its head and stepped forward once, and then again.

Adelaide paused as the dog let out a low, uneasy growl. "Easy, there. I won't hurt you." She held one hand out. She took another slow step through the underbrush toward the strange cyborg dog.

Darius held his breath. He wanted to tell her to stop, but she looked so confident, so sure of herself.

"She shouldn't be—" the woman started.

"Oh," Adelaide said suddenly.

"What is it?" Darius asked.

"It's eyes. I hadn't really seen them before. It's like they're made of tinted glass."

"They're camera lenses." The woman sighed as stepped toward Adelaide and the creature.

The dog looked at the woman, and Darius could sense the distrust.

"Easy, pup. What's the dog's name?" Adelaide asked.

"Its designation is B3661A-1. It's a Cy-warg."

"See? That's part of your problem," Adelaide said to the woman. She turned back to the dog. "You aren't a designation, no, you're a good dog who was trying to make someone proud. You're mad at her, and you can sense her guilt. Can't you? She feels bad leaving you out here."

"She's not wrong," Darius chimed in. He wanted to tell Adelaide to stop, to be careful, but he also wanted a better look at the creature. And Adelaide looked magnificent.

"Is the dog a boy or a girl?" Adelaide asked.

"It was a male dog," the woman replied warily.

"Then he's a he, not an it, aren't you? Come on, boy," Adelaide coaxed. Her tone was even and soothing.

The creature padded toward Adelaide.

The woman stiffened.

The dog was right up next to Adelaide now. He

moved his snout toward her hand.

Adelaide smiled. "Hello there, I'm Adelaide."

Darius held his breath.

The dog sniffed Adelaide's hand.

"You should have a name, too. I think—" Adelaide looked at the dog "—we could call you, Barkly. Would you like that?"

The dog wagged its tail and nudged Adelaide's hand with its metal nose.

"Well, all right then," Adelaide said as she scratched the fur between his ears. "Barkly it is."

"If it's all the same to you," the woman said to Adelaide, "we should leave now." She eyed the dog warily.

It looked toward the woman and let out another low growl in response.

"It seems smart," Darius said, as he observed the dog. "I'm not sure it likes you."

"It's as smart as a ten-year-old," the woman boasted. "I know, I made it. I didn't realize it would get so carried away, though."

Adelaide wheeled on her. Her voice remained flat, but her eyes blazed. "You transformed this creature to be something you wanted, and it did its job, and then you abandoned it out in the woods. It was probably scared and confused. Any ten-year-old would be if you left them out here."

The woman recoiled and blinked, dumbfounded.

Barkly tensed.

"You have to greet him. Like you said, he's smart." Adelaide's voice softened. "And you aren't his boss." She turned back to Barkly and stroked his head.

"I—" The woman looked between Adelaide and the dog. "I really am sorry, Barkly. I shouldn't have left you here." She held out her hand.

Barkly stopped growling, padded forward and sniffed the woman's hand.

"So, uh, I mean we kind of helped you out ..." Darius trailed off. He wondered how far they could push their luck. "What, I mean is, it senses guilt I guess, but what was the point of Barkly's ... umm, transformations?"

The woman pursed her lips.

Darius could sense she was about to tell them to go home again. He crossed his fingers, hoping they could glean some other piece of information before they left.

Adelaide stroked the dog's head and the woman sighed and began to speak. "Look, it, I mean, he, was a prototype I was working on. It failed. I didn't have the heart to put him down, so I released him."

"But then he started attacking people," Darius prodded.

The woman glanced warily at the dog. "He was just doing his job," she admitted to Darius.

"Does this have anything to do with the birds?" Darius pressed. He glanced toward Barkly who continued to enjoy Adelaide's ministrations.

"The birds?" the woman asked confused.

"The ones that keep being aggressive," Adelaide explained. "The ones Grover Jergen was working on."

"Oh." The woman blinked. "No, no." She hesitated. "This, he,"—she gestured toward Barkley— "is a very different project. I designed him to assist law enforcement. He has improved senses, enhanced physical attributes, and limited precognitive function." She looked at them. "Barkly can sense guilt. I was supposed to put him down because he mauled my lab partner. It seems he'd been cheating on his spouse and felt a lot of guilt about it."

Darius' eyes widened at the thought of someone being mauled by a dog after being unfaithful.

The woman tentatively stroked Barkly's head.

"Can you tell us anything about Grover Jergen's birds?" Adelaide asked. Her hand fell to her side as she let the woman take over petting Barkly.

"What?" the woman asked, obviously distracted with the dog.

"You seemed to know about him," Darius pushed.

The woman sighed. "We both worked at The Link, okay? I'm really not supposed to talk about it. None of us are."

"Because they'll kill you?" Darius asked. He imagined facilities with secret projects like this would go to great lengths to keep their secrets.

"No! Because we sign NDAs," the woman said with a frown. "Dr. Jergen was experimenting on birds. It was a very different project than," she paused, "Barkly here. I don't know much about Dr. Jergen. We didn't really talk. I like to keep to myself."

Darius sighed in frustration. "Can't you tell us anything about him? Where is he? How do we stop his crazy birds?"

"No offense, because I appreciate the help, but you two are kids. You should be riding bikes or playing ball, not getting involved in anything to do with The Link or the people who work there." She raised her eyebrows at the two of them.

"Look—" Darius started.

"Hey, it's okay," Adelaide said as she put a hand on Darius' arm. "We figured this out and that's something."

Darius felt a bit better with that. He took a breath and decided to try a different tactic. "What are you going to do with Barkly now? He can't stay here."

"But you have to find a good home for him," Adelaide added as she looked at the woman, then down at Barkly. "He's a good dog."

"I'll move somewhere rural, I suppose," the woman said with a sigh. "I didn't feel right leaving him out here. I just didn't know what else to do. I didn't want them to destroy him."

"Then you have to keep telling him that." Adelaide gestured toward the creature. "If he's as smart as you say, he understands you. I hate when people treat me like I'm stupid because I'm a kid."

The woman nodded. "I suppose you would."

***

Adelaide drained the pot of pasta into a colander in the sink. A cloud of steam filled the air.

Darius hovered nearby. "That was totally rad. I can't believe we found it, or him I mean. The dog. You were awesome!"

"Oh, thanks," Adelaide said as she shook the colander. Little streams of water escaped from the holes in the bottom. She was still processing what she'd seen in the forest. "I can't believe stuff like that is around here and I never noticed."

"You didn't notice *before,* but now you've got a knack for sniffing it out. We make a great team," Darius said with a grin. "This place really is rad. So much better than Boston."

Adelaide turned and gave him a small smile. His enthusiasm was infectious.

"It's too bad about the birds," Darius said. "I want to know more."

"Me too, but I don't think we have any other leads. Dr. Jergen left town and it's too far away for us to bike to. Plus, those birds, if they were some of his, were pretty vicious," Adelaide pointed out. "I'm not sure there's much we can do except hope they fly to wherever he is. And there's a chance those agents from the haunted house found him."

"I suppose so," Darius replied. A shadow of frustration crossed his face.

"Hey, we still solved the mystery of the dog."

"That's true," Darius said, brightening. "Do you think she'll do it? Take care of Barkly?" he asked.

"I hope so." Adelaide said as she dumped the pasta back into the pot, added a glob of margarine, a splash of milk, and a package of cheese powder. She stirred until the mixture was an even shade of bright yellow.

She had liked Barkly on sight. For just a moment she wondered what it would be like to bring him home, but it never would have worked, not with the people who lived here.

"Me, too." Darius' voice broke her from her reverie.

"Darius?" Adelaide asked.

"Yeah?" His voice was cheerful.

She pursed her lips. "Why'd you attack her? We were all just talking and then you attacked her."

Darius' face clouded and he looked down at his feet. "I'm sorry ..."

Adelaide's heart sank at how upset Darius looked. She thought about saying it didn't matter, but it did. She needed some sort of explanation.

Darius took a deep breath. "You were in danger and I didn't want ..." he trailed off as he looked up. "Something just came over me. It isn't the first time it's happened."

"Your last school?" Adelaide guessed. She thought about how she'd seen Darius clench his fists around Tetsu.

Darius nodded, then looked back down at the floor. "I …" he trailed off again, unable to summon the words he was looking for.

"Darius?" Adelaide asked gently. She never felt in danger around him, and he'd never taken a swing at Tetsu.

He looked up at her again. His face was awash with regret and looked unfamiliar without his usual carefree grin. "Yeah?"

"I'm your friend. I'm here for you"—she put her hand lightly on his arm—"but you don't have to tell me if you aren't ready, or don't want to."

Darius nodded, and a hint of his usual spark returned.

"Please just be a bit more careful in future, okay?" Adelaide requested as she stirred the pot of pasta again. She set down the wooden spoon and collected three bowls from the cupboard.

"Adelaide?" Darius asked.

She set the bowls on the counter and turned her attention back to him. "Yes?"

"I beat up a kid. Really badly. He went to the hospital," Darius said. He met her eyes and searched them.

"Why did you do it?" Adelaide asked, certain he must have had a reason.

"He was picking on another kid, Quinton. Like, a lot. Quinton, he wasn't my friend exactly, but he, he didn't deserve that. No one does. No one else stepped in. Not even the teachers. They didn't notice," Darius explained. "And then ..." He trailed off again as a haunted expression crossed his face. "I snapped."

Adelaide studied him, absorbing the information. She could see the worry on his face, the concern in his eyes. Adelaide knew he was done talking about it and she knew all she needed to. She nodded. "Okay. If you ever want to talk about it, I promise I'm here." She fished a fork out of the drawer, scooped a piece of pasta onto it, and handed it to Darius. "What do you think?"

Adelaide watched Darius take a bite of the Kraft Macaroni and Cheese.

He chewed and swallowed. "It's, ah, different."

"I can't believe you've never had Kraft mac and cheese." Adelaide shook her head. She portioned the pasta into three bowls. "Oh, here. You can't forget the ketchup. My mom says that's the vegetable." She handed him the bottle and indicated toward the table.

"Ketchup is not a vegetable," Darius protested.

"Pardon me?" Belinda asked as she entered the kitchen. She was dressed in jeans and a shirt that clung to her figure. Her hair was fluffed and coiffed to perfection. She bobbed to the rhythm of The Cure's "Boys Don't Cry" from the speaker in the other room.

"Hi Mrs. Winter. I'm just saying it's not really a vegetable." Darius flushed and ran his hand through his hair.

"It's *Ms.* Winter, and it certainly is." Belinda took the ketchup and squirted a smiley face onto her bowl of bright yellow macaroni. She pointed at the bottle. "See, there's a tomato right there."

"Just go with it," Adelaide murmured.

"My mistake, I see," Darius replied.

"Thanks for making dinner, baby," Belinda said. She smiled as the three of them took a seat at the table.

Darius slid in next to Adelaide on the bench.

"Darius has never had Kraft mac and cheese before."

"What?" Belinda put her fork down. "How can this be?" She gaped. "Get out. You'll have to leave."

Darius chuckled.

"Rico is coming by tonight." Belinda wiggled her eyebrows at Adelaide.

"Is he?" Adelaide asked.

Darius looked between the two of them. It seemed like such a strange conversation to have with a parent.

"Yes, he promised." Belinda smiled. She lifted a forkful of pasta to her mouth.

"Okay."

"He's a pretty great boyfriend, right baby?" Belinda asked after she'd swallowed the bite.

"What do I know about boyfriends, Mama?" Adelaide replied. She lifted her own forkful of pasta to her mouth.

"Oh, I'm sure you know something," Belinda murmured with a smile.

The rest of the dinner was pleasant and filled with friendly banter. Darius found it a far cry from his own family dinners.

"We'll wash the dishes, Mama," Adelaide said as they finished eating. "Then maybe you can drive Darius home?"

"Sounds great, baby," Belinda said with a smile. She stood up from the table and placed her bowl and the sink. "You're welcome back any time, Darius. But you'll have to remember that in this house, ketchup is a vegetable."

"Sure thing, Ms. Winter," Darius replied.

Belinda turned and left the kitchen.

Adelaide filled the sink with hot water and a squirt of dish soap. She could feel Darius' eyes on her as she watched the bubbles pile higher atop the surface of the water.

"What is it?" she asked as she turned to look at him.

"Ketchup isn't a vegetable," Darius said.

Adelaide opened her mouth to respond when Darius grinned.

"I'll pretend it is, though, if it means more time with you."

Adelaide smiled shyly and nodded. "Do you want to wash or dry?"

Sixteen

Ray closed the backdoor of the car and shook his head. The backseat was covered in computers, monitors and floppy discs. The floor of the backseat was littered with medical grade gloves, masks, syringes, and assorted labeled and unlabeled vials. He turned back to the dilapidated trailer.

"I think that's all of it," Ray called as he climbed the rickety steps.

"Good," Gary said. "This guy is nuts."

"And we're sure he didn't leave any research with anyone?" Ray asked as he entered the trailer.

"The man's nuts," Gary repeated. "And this project is even crazier. Controlling the birds? Good luck with that. Who'd want to be a part of it?"

"Yes, I suppose we've all seen *The Birds,*" Ray replied with a shudder. He glanced around at the mobile domicile Dr. Grover Jergen had come to call home for the last few months. It was a sad place that was sadder still now that they'd ransacked it. Grover Jergen was tied to an old kitchen chair.

"I don't like bird watching," Gary said.

Ray blinked.

Gary reached down and repositioned the gag in Grover Jergen's mouth.

The scientist's cheek was red and had started to swell.

"Did you hit him?" Ray turned to his partner.

"So what? He's a raving lunatic. He talks nonsense. You know what this place looked like." Gary gestured with his gun.

A lot of the trailer's contents had been loaded into their vehicle already, but when they'd arrived, the tin can was a mess. Bird feathers, streaks of blood, operating equipment, and microchips the doctor had been inserting into his test subjects.

"He's still a person."

Doctor Jergen twitched in the chair. His eyes darted between the two men. He tried to speak, but the gag muffled him beyond comprehension.

"He is literally a mad scientist," Gary retorted. "Look, we all know how this is going to go."

"It doesn't have to," Ray replied.

"Edmunds couldn't handle it. That's why we're

here. This is what we do." Gary pulled his pistol from its holster. "It's the last flight of the bird man."

Ray pursed his lips as Gary pulled the trigger. This was the part of the job he hated.

***

Adelaide and Tetsu started down her driveway toward the bus stop. She glanced up at the grey sky. It hadn't started to rain. Yet.

"I didn't tell you!" Tetsu exclaimed.

"Tell me what?" Adelaide asked.

"I talked to Reggie and Colin. I was right—they had nothing to do with Mrs. Anders' car," Tetsu gloated.

"Do they know who did?" Adelaide asked.

"Yes," Tetsu admitted.

"So, I was right, too?" Adelaide teased.

"Fine. Yes, you were right, too," Tetsu admitted.

"Who was it?" Adelaide asked as the two of them proceeded down the street.

"The Puffin brothers. Bruce and Bradley Puffin. Plus their little minion Dillon."

"Of course, it was." Adelaide shook her head. "I like that you call him a minion, by the way. He's older and bigger than you."

"He's minion material," Tetsu said with a wave of his hand.

"What are you going to do?" Adelaide asked.

"Nothing. I mean, I can't tell Mrs. Anders. For one, I'm not a snitch. And two, she won't believe me anyway. I'd end up in more trouble."

Adelaide nodded in agreement. "If only grownups listened," she mused. "We know so much more than they give us credit for."

Tetsu laughed and Adelaide cracked a small smile.

Kurt exited his house and walked at a normal speed toward them.

Adelaide turned her smile to Kurt. Some days were better than others in the Zillman house. She always wished there was more she could do for Kurt, but in all the years as friends, the best she'd come up with was to just be there. "Everything okay this morning?"

Kurt nodded. "Yes, how's your house this morning?"

Adelaide frowned. "Rico's over. I caught him drinking orange juice right out of the carton. Again."

"That's nasty," Tetsu said. "I only do that with soda."

Kurt shook his head in disgust.

"Oh, I saw a part robot dog," Adelaide added.

Kurt's eyes widened. "No way! How much of it was robotic? Was it a cyborg?"

"You went without me?" Tetsu scowled. "This is what you do now? Put yourself in danger to look at freaky stuff?"

"Tetsu." Adelaide looked at him. "I'm okay. I promise." She wondered if that was why he'd acted so strangely the day before. He'd been worried. "Why don't I fill everyone in at once?" Adelaide suggested as Sophie bounded down her front steps.

Adelaide recounted the previous day's excitement as they walked to the bus stop.

"What happens now?" Sophie asked as the bus pulled up.

"Nothing, I suppose," Tetsu said. "Hopefully she takes him somewhere and we never see them again."

Adelaide nodded in agreement. She frowned slightly at Tetsu, certain there was something he wasn't saying. She decided not to press the matter.

"I wish I'd at least gotten to see it," Kurt said.

Tetsu balked.

"Sit with me Kurt!" Julie called as they stepped on the bus.

Sophie and Kurt both froze, confused by the sudden turn of events. Adelaide slipped into her usual seat and Tetsu flopped dejected next to her.

"Um," Kurt said as he looked between the bench behind Adelaide and the one several rows down. "Okay?" He avoided eye contact with Sophie as he walked toward Julie.

"What world is this?" Sophie huffed as she flopped into Kurt's usual seat alone. "This is supposed to be *my* year."

"I warned ya," Tetsu murmured. "Things are changing."

"Maybe change isn't always a bad thing," Adelaide mused. Despite worrying about Tetsu, she felt warm inside thinking about her adventure with Darius.

"Are you smiling?" Tetsu gawked.

"Maybe I am," Adelaide replied in an even tone.

"What world is this?" Tetsu mumbled.

"I *just* asked that," Sophie lamented.

Adelaide turned to look out the window at houses as they went by. Her friends weren't wrong; the world was different now, but different didn't mean bad.

Olympic Vista Chronicles

Everything twelve-year-old Adelaide Winter knows about her Washington state hometown is turned on its head when Darius Belcouer moves to Olympic Vista at the end of summer 1986.

The two become fast friends as they bond over the mystery of a local haunted house Darius wants to explore. The house, it turns out, is only the tip of the iceberg. They quickly discover the more they dig, the more they uncover, and the trail leads back to The Link, a research and development facility in town. Together, Adelaide and her friends delve into the strange occurrences around Olympic Vista.

A tale of friendship, horror, and coming of age in the late 80s.

Coming Soon:
Costumes & Copiers

October has arrived in Olympic Vista. Pumpkins decorate the doorsteps and the crisp autumn air carries a promise of Halloween treats, but the small town is never without a few tricks.

When the copy centre Adelaide's mother works at disappears overnight, Adelaide and her friends become determined to find out what really happened.

And, as Halloween draws closer, children of all ages flock to Dizzy's Halloween Emporium for "the best fright-ses for the lowest prices." Will Adelaide and Darius be able to cohost another successful party? Or will the strange happenings of Olympic Vista prove to be more than they can handle?

About the Author

Kelly Pawlik dabbled with story writing from a young age. She spent her childhood reading, dressing her beloved cat, Midnight, up in doll clothes, and hunting garter snakes in the backyard. Her childhood dream was to be an author and she is proud to be bringing character to life with her Olympic Vista Chronicles novellas.

Kelly is a tabletop roleplaying game (TTRPG) writer and has released multiple RPG supplements with her husband under their micro-publishing company, Dire

Rugrat Publishing. She has also contributed to several best-selling works with Kobold Press.

Kelly lives on Vancouver Island, BC with her husband, their three inquisitive children, and two lazy cats.

You can follow Kelly on:

Facebook: kellypawlikauthor
Instagram: kellypawlikauthor
Twitter: @KellyPawlik84

Sign up to receive Kelly's newsletter and you'll get access to sneak peeks of upcoming novellas, behind the scenes information and other exclusive content including bonus scenes and short stories.

Visit her website at olympicvistapublishing.com for more information.